THE INCENDIARY MURDERS

DI GILES BOOK 20

ANNA-MARIE MORGAN

For Jean and Christopher, with my love

ALSO BY ANNA-MARIE MORGAN

1

EXPLOSIVE BEGINNINGS

The van pulled up at the gates of a large estate, its driver tapping the steering wheel, eyes shielded from view and the harsh spring sun by dark glasses; window wide open. Music pulsed from the radio he had turned down so he could talk.

Ted was in no hurry. Due to be relieved at any moment, the fifty-three-year-old security guard flicked away his cigarette, and pushed his shades up on his head.

His colleague Pete's voice came over the radio. "Mate, I'm gonna be another five minutes."

"What, again?" He sighed.

"It can't be helped. Call of nature. You know how it is?"

Ted tutted. "Typical... Yeah, no problem, mate. We got someone at the gates. Looks like a delivery. I'll sort it while you powder your nose."

"I really am sorry, mate..."

"Don't worry about it."

The van driver leaned his head out of the window, making a big thing of looking at his watch. "Sometime today would be good?" He grinned to soften the dig. "Some of us have places to go."

Ted checked his own timepiece. He would have to deal with the delivery. Another delay in getting off work, but not enough overtime to warrant extra pay.

He took the keys out of his pocket, turning them in the lock of the twelve-foot-high iron gates. The button for the automatic mechanism had gone on the blink one day prior. It was one of those weeks.

The delivery guy stopped tapping and put his vehicle in gear.

Ted pulled the gates open one at a time and waved the man in. He couldn't see through the guy's sunglasses. He didn't trust it when he couldn't read an expression. Ted stopped the driver when the van was half-way through the gates.

"Delivery for a Mr Rothwell?" The man scanned his clipboard. "Several packages, one of them is a two-person carry." He looked up from his instructions. "It says here to take them up to the house."

Ted narrowed his eyes, leaning in through the window. "Lemme see…"

The explosion splayed the van; left the gates hanging off their hinges; rocked the security hut and smashed or cracked the windows of the gardener's cottage halfway to the main house.

Ted's charred remains had been blown several feet, while the van burned with billowing black smoke and orange-red flame.

Inside the gardener's cottage, Pete soaked his trouser front, running from the building.

Shaking, he stared open-mouthed at the carnage. "Shit!"

He ran towards the burning vehicle, falling back from

the searing heat and choking fumes. He swivelled his head, looking for his colleague. "Fuck!" Ted's blackened body was still smoking. He knelt next to it, feeling the left side of his friend's throat. A lump formed in his own. Ted was gone, and so too was Pete's ability to reason.

He stood, heart banging against his ribs, legs trembling so much he thought they might collapse. "Pull yourself together!" He fished out his mobile phone.

Another smaller explosion sent him ducking to the ground, rolling over and over to put some distance between himself and the stricken van. The fuel could go up at any moment.

It was almost impossible, relaying what had happened to a patient operator, while his tongue stuck to the roof of his mouth. Words wouldn't form, his brain still trying to work out what the hell had happened; processing the death of his friend.

Beyond the wrecked gates, two or three people had gathered.

As Pete put his mobile away, an onlooker talked on theirs while the others used phones to film the destruction. Any other time, and he would have shooed the ghoulish viewers away, but not today. The presence of other human beings was reassuring as he waited for the cacophony of approaching sirens to arrive.

He ran a trembling hand through his thinning hair, still coming to terms with what he had witnessed. What in God's name had just happened?

～

YVONNE AND DEWI arrived at Riverdale Mansion, situated off the main road to Shrewsbury, near Welshpool. Emergency personnel were busy with the smouldering wreckage, assessing the mangled remains of the van and the bodies of the deceased.

Firefighters had hosed down the area, putting out the remaining fire.

SOCO officers photographed the dead security guard before placing a body bag next to his remains. Other officers measured the distance from his body to the van, discussing the damage to the charred corpse of the driver.

The control room operator had given the DI only the bare bones of the situation that greeted them on their arrival.

"Delivery van explosion; at least one fatality," she had said.

As Yvonne surveyed the scene before her, she knew it had been the understatement of the year. Nausea gripped her as the smell of burned flesh stung her nostrils. She stifled a gag.

"Are you okay?" Dewi was at her elbow. "It's a helluva a scene." He sighed. "I don't know what I expected, but it wasn't this."

She pressed her lips together, straightening her back. "It looks like a bomb went off, perhaps on a timer?" Her eyes travelled to the enormous porticoed mansion, with Doric and Corinthian pillars and Georgian sash windows. "Who lives there? Do we know?"

Dewi shielded his eyes from the sun. "That is Dean Rothwell's place."

She frowned. "Dean Rothwell? Why does that name ring a bell?"

"You don't know Rothwell? He's rock royalty... He's getting on in years now, but his band, The Stoney Bastions, still pulls a sizeable crowd when they play the smaller stadiums."

"The Stoney Bastions? That's an unusual name."

"Apparently they were going to call themselves something else, referring to out-of-it fatherless children. Their manager suggested the name would put radio stations off playing their music, so they toned it down."

The DI's eyes returned to the blackened body of the dead security guard. "I bet the poor bugger didn't expect this when he turned up for work this morning. What is happening to our world, Dewi?"

Her sergeant shook his head. "It's not the sort of thing we expect to happen around here. I should think they'll want the big boys on this. It reeks of organised crime." He pursed his lips. "Perhaps the gangs are extending their grip."

"Maybe..." The DI cast her eyes around for the second security guard, which the operator had told her was still on scene. She guessed he was the individual with a foil blanket around his shoulders; speaking with a paramedic, and shivering despite the arid heat of the June day. "I'll catch up with you later, Dewi. I want a chat with the other guard; ask him what happened."

"Right-oh, I'll pop over to the house and look around."

"Good idea," she said, turning her attention back to the wide-eyed man being examined by the ambulance crew. Although an important part of her job, asking a shell-shocked witness questions so soon after a major incident felt uncomfortable. She pressed her lips together, clearing her throat. The best time was now, while the memories were fresh; unembellished by the frequent retelling that was bound to follow.

He appeared lost, staring through her.

Yvonne could tell he was reliving the moments during

and after the explosion. "Pete?" She tilted her head, waiting for his eyes to focus on her face. "Pete Davies?"

"That's me." He came to with a start. "I'm Pete Davies."

"My name is Yvonne Giles. I'm a DI with Dyfed-Powys police. I was hoping you could tell me what happened here?"

A paramedic handed a bottle of water to the security guard, giving the DI a nod before heading back to his colleagues.

Pete gulped some down; wiping his mouth before answering. "I don't really know." He pointed to a small hut along the lane, half-way to the Riverdale Mansion. "I was in there, needing a leak. I was only in there a minute, and I heard this massive explosion. It cracked the windows. I ran outside and couldn't believe my eyes. And... and Ted was lying there, not moving. I checked his pulse, but he was gone. I could see that even before I felt his neck. Perhaps I should have tried CPR, maybe I could have made a difference, but I panicked. I didn't think I would, but I did. I've done this job for many years, and... and nothing like this has ever happened before."

"It would have been a shock for anyone. I'm not surprised you froze."

"I did, I froze. But... but it should have been me, you see."

"I don't understand?" The DI scoured his face.

"I should have been on duty five minutes before the van went up. So, I apologised to Ted and told him I was running late and needed a pee. I was supposed to have taken over from him, and it should have been me opening the gate for the deliveries." He looked over to the forensic officers processing the dead guard's body. "It ought to be me lying there, not Ted." He brought his eyes back to hers. "He was a good man; one of the best. He did not deserve this."

She gave a slow blink to show she understood. "Pete, did you see the van approach the gates?"

He nodded. "I saw it through the window when I entered the hut."

"What speed was it doing?"

"A few miles an hour, nothing out of the ordinary. I watched it until it stopped at the gates, waiting to be let through. When I saw it approaching, I radioed through to Ted to let him know I was going to be a few minutes late relieving him. So he knew to stay and let the van in. Hell, we have let delivery drivers through those gates many a time. I still can't believe this. It is surreal. Rhonda, Ted's wife, will be beside herself. And his kids... He has two youngsters, a boy and a girl. His family will be devastated. I don't think they know yet."

Yvonne nodded. "Specialist officers will inform and support them. They will get all the help we can give. But, yes, it will be a horrible shock for them. It's going to be a difficult few months." She rubbed her chin. "How was Ted this morning? Was he out of sorts at all?"

Pete scratched his head. "No, he was the same as always. We had the usual banter over who was going to brew the cuppa. That was first thing this morning, before we split up. Ted manned the gates, and I checked the house over. He was getting off early this afternoon. Otherwise, when I took over gate duty, he would normally have been in charge of the house."

"Do you know of anyone who might wish harm on either of you or on the owner of the house?"

"Rothwell, you mean? No, not really... I can't imagine why anyone would have wanted to harm either myself or Ted, but Rothwell? Well, I can't comment on that, really. He moves in different circles, like. I suppose he must meet an awful lot of different people with his rockstar lifestyle."

"Do you know where he is?"

"He is away on tour. He is in the country, but I couldn't tell you the order of the venues he and his band are playing at. Ted was usually the one who kept up with that sort of stuff. But, if you look him up online, I daresay you'll find all that out. We have the numbers you can get him on, though. I have his mobile number on my work phone. Hang on..." He rooted in his pocket, pulling it out. "We can contact him in emergencies. I should have called him earlier, but I couldn't think beyond dialling the emergency services."

"It is going to take a while for all this to sink in." Yvonne nodded. "You did very well. No-one is going to judge you for not calling your employer right away. Perhaps you should call your wife. Let her know you are okay. This will soon hit the news, if it hasn't already. She will be beside herself with worry if she hasn't heard from you."

He fished out another phone. "Oh, God... I've missed five calls from her." He grimaced. "I leave my personal mobile on silent between break times. I better call her."

"You do that." She turned her attention to a firefighter who was removing his helmet to mop a brow blackened by soot.

The DI approached him as he drank water from a bottle supplied by a paramedic. "I apologise. I can see you are taking a well-deserved break, but do you have any idea what happened here? Was this a bomb?"

His eyes narrowed. "I'm sorry, I-"

"Yvonne Giles." She showed him her badge. "I'm a DI from Newtown."

"Ah." He grinned. "I thought for a moment you were a

reporter. We have to be careful not to release unverified information, as you know."

"Absolutely."

He set down his helmet and sat on the verge, regarding her as he drank more water. "At first glance, it looks to have been a fairly crude device... basic circuitry wired to a chemical mix. To know more, we'll obviously need lab analysis, but it could have been fertiliser-based."

"I see." She scanned the crowd gathered at the cordon beyond the smashed gates. "Can you tell if it was in a parcel?"

He shrugged. "Any packaging was demolished when it went off. We only have the metallic remnants of the circuit, and the melted remains of what was probably the chemical container. There's a lot of sifting and sorting to be done before we can reconstruct the device."

"I see." She nodded. "Thank you. I'll let you get on with your break."

❧

SPOTTING Dewi on the front steps of Riverdale, she strode over to him.

"The house is empty," he informed her. "Rothwell and his entourage are away on tour."

"Are they out of the country?" Why ask? He told you no.

He shook his head. "They played Milton Keynes last night. Rothwell has cancelled tonight's show, and is on his way back here." Dewi pursed his lips. "The dead security guard, Ted Edwards, was his longest-serving employee. The star says he is gutted at the loss."

"Was Rothwell due home soon? Was he expecting a parcel to be delivered today?"

Dewi shrugged. "I guess we can ask him when he arrives back. The guards were the only people here today."

Yvonne scratched her chin. "Whoever sent the device must have expected him home, or the bomb was triggered when it shouldn't have been."

"You suppose it was meant for Rothwell?" Dewi frowned. "What if it wasn't?"

"You have a point. Just because he is a high-profile individual, doesn't mean the bomb was meant for him. But, if not, why go to all this trouble? To damage the house? Kill the security guards? Scare him? A quick internet search would have told the bomber the star wouldn't be home. It makes no sense."

"Maybe it was supposed to intimidate Rothwell?"

"Perhaps, but it was a lot of effort and risk if the only aim was to make the singer feel uncomfortable."

"I guess we'll have to wait until we hear what Rothwell has to say. Perhaps he received threats prior to this, although I asked our control room to look into it, and they said nothing had been reported."

"Has Rothwell been in trouble before?"

"He has a history of mostly minor stuff, like drug possession and criminal damage. But there was a common assault and domestic violence incident some years ago. He has trashed a few hotel rooms in his time, mind. Four decades ago, he was rarely off the front pages."

The DI nodded. "We'll take a thorough look through his record. Maybe he upset someone. But first, we need the identity of the van driver, and to talk to the company he worked for. They should have records for the packages and who sent them. We'll start there."

2

AN INTRICATE WEB

The following morning, Yvonne and Dewi were back on the steps of Riverdale, looking out across well-kept grounds and mature landscaping. Their beauty was at odds with the mangled gates and lines of police tape surrounding the crime scene. Forensic personnel were still working hard to establish exactly what happened.

In the distance, as they waited for the door to be answered, they could hear the thrum of a ride-on lawn mower. The gardener was continuing his daily routine only two hundred metres from where the tragedy had taken place.

"Sorry about all that." A sixty-something male appeared in the doorway, his lower face peppered with grey stubble. Dressed in a plain white tee shirt and jeans, the short-haired, wiry man held out his hand. "I'm Dean. I'm the guy who owns this place." After shaking their hands, he ran his fingers through short-cropped hair, sighing. "Come this way. We're in the main sitting room trying to work out what happened out there."

There was a raspiness to his voice, and the DI detected a tremor in the hand which had shaken hers. It was hard to know whether this was shock, nerves, or Rothwell coming down off some substance or other.

He led them into a large drawing room filled with the light from four enormous sash windows that faced the road leading to the house. The pale-grey wall colour, stuccoed ceiling, and art styled after the old masters gave a serenity to their surroundings. Their peaceful ambience was at odds with the tension in the hunched, pacing friends and band members around the room.

"Would you like a drink of something?" A leggy blonde in a red sleeveless dress, around thirty years Rothwell's junior, held up a half-filled wineglass.

Yvonne raised a hand. "No, thank you. We're on duty."

Rothwell placed an arm around the woman's shoulders, giving her a quick squeeze and a pat on the backside, before leaving her to wander over to the windows. "Look at the mess." He placed his hands on his hips. "What the heck happened?" The singer sighed. "I don't get it. Who on earth would do something like this?"

"We were hoping you might have some ideas?" Yvonne scoured the others in the room, six not including the Rothwell's girlfriend. Five males and another female who sat huddled with a long-haired older man.

"I'm DI Yvonne Giles, and this is DS Dewi Hughes," she began. "We're here to ask you questions about yesterday's tragic events."

"Yes, I guessed as much." Rothwell turned from the window. "Well, I'm Dean Rothwell, and this is Andy, Trev, Dave, and Simes." He pointed to each of the seated males before indicating another man pacing the floor. "And that's my mate, Jase."

"Could we have everyone's full names?" Dewi asked, pen to paper.

"Er, yeah, sure." Rothwell began with the seated males. "My band members: Andrew Walsh, Trevor Morris, Dave Todd, and Simon Mason." He pointed to the male who had ceased wearing down the carpet. "That is my mate Jason Leyland, and the blonde lady over there is my girlfriend, the lovely Jeanette Dupont, otherwise known as Jeanie. The redhead with her is Trev's girlfriend, Pattie Caldwell. I think that's everybody."

"Thank you." Dewi scribbled it down.

"It must have been quite a shock when you heard about this yesterday?" Yvonne cocked her head, her eyes on Rothwell's face.

"You can say that again... I was stunned. I'm still stunned. I can't get my head round it." The singer's cockney accent deepened as he spoke, running a hand over short-cropped hair, his mouth hanging open for dramatic effect. "I mean, it's not every day someone drives a bomb to your door and detonates it in your garden, is it? Look at the state out there. I tell you, when I find out who it is, I'll kill 'em."

The DI cleared her throat. "I understand Ted was one of your longest-serving employees?"

"Oh, yeah... Ted..." Rothwell grimaced. "He's got a wife and kids. The kids are grown-up now, but still... You don't go to work expecting that sort of thing to happen, do you? Rhonda, that's his wife, must be devastated. They'd been married thirty years."

Yvonne examined the faces of the other people in the room. Andy, with long grey-hair in a ponytail, sat with his eyes half-lidded, lost in his own thoughts. Bald-headed, thick-set Trev sat back on the sofa, arm around his partner, staring at the floor. Dave, also long-haired, in a tee shirt and a denim jacket with studs and frayed armholes, looked to be falling asleep. And short-haired Simes sat fidgeting, his ankle moving up and down, as he chewed the inside of his cheek. Jeanette continued drowning her sorrows in a glass, and the red-haired Patti was busy shrinking into Trevor Morris's armpit.

The DI knew if she tipped Dewi the nod, he would usher out the entourage, leaving her alone to question Rothwell without distraction. But for now, she wanted them together to observe their interactions and facial expressions as she talked with the singer. So far, they appeared to have retreated into inner worlds while they processed the events of the day before.

"Mr Rothwell, were you expecting a parcel delivery yesterday?"

He shook his head. "No."

"Are you sure about that?"

He shrugged. "I sometimes have things sent to me by fans, but as for ordering something, absolutely not. I wasn't due home for another week, so although I have sent for things to be delivered while I was away in the past, I didn't this time."

"When you have done so on previous occasions, did the house security staff accept packages on your behalf?"

"Well yeah, of course. Ted and Pete have taken deliveries for me many times over the years."

"And you would remember ordering something more recently?"

"Sure, how could I forget if I had just bought something?"

"What if you had been drinking at the time?"

"I would still remember."

"Who might have sent these parcels to your address?

Could it have been a fan, or has anyone else said they might send you a gift?"

He shook his head. "I can't think of anyone who would have sent stuff to me this week."

"Have you been threatened recently, in person or by letter?"

"Not that I can recall, no."

"I'm sure you would remember if you had?"

"Yeah, it would be hard to forget something like that." Rothwell looked across the room to his girlfriend, who was still supping wine. "I mean, we have drunken banter sometimes. Who doesn't? But I haven't been seriously threatened by anyone recently."

"Recently? Are you saying you've received threats in the past?"

He nodded towards his girlfriend. "Your ex said he'd do me in a couple of years ago, didn't he?"

Jeanie nodded, her wide-eyes gazing over the rim of her glass.

"When was the last time you had contact with this ex?" Yvonne looked from one to the other of them.

"Oh, let's see… Not for a while…" Rothwell frowned.

"How long is a while?"

"I don't know… A year? Eighteen months?"

"Who is the ex, and where does he live?"

"His name is Mark Wiggins, and he's in London as far as we know. He wasn't happy when Jeanie left him for me, but he's got a new woman, and I don't think he would try to blow us up after all this time."

"Have you argued with anyone else recently? Or engaged in a social media war, for example?"

He shook his head. "I use social media, but I haven't

been on there in a while. Our manager is usually the one who responds to messages and posts."

"I see." She pursed her lips. "Is there anyone else you know who could have done this to you?"

"Nobody I can think of."

"Very well." The DI rose from her seat. "I will probably need to speak to you again soon. Will you be around?"

Rothwell rubbed his chin. "My manager wants to discuss the rest of the tour with me later today. We may cancel shows for the next few weeks. I don't really know what to do for the best. I don't enjoy disappointing fans but, after what has happened... I'm sure they will understand."

"I'm sure they will." The DI nodded. "And you will appreciate the downtime, to clear your head and process these events and the death of Ted. Give yourselves some time."

"Hang on, I'll see you out." Rothwell stood. "I gave Pete the day off. The other staff were not due back until next month, but I have asked them to come back next week."

"Who are the other staff?" The DI paused in the doorway.

"The housekeeper, Madge Lawson; the cook, Trish Jones; and the cleaner, Helen Jameson."

"So, you have five house staff, including the security guards?"

"Well, there is the gardener, Derek Davies, but he comes and goes when he needs to, including while I am away. The female staff are only usually here when we are home, starting the day before we return from tour."

"Got it." She nodded. "Officers will speak to your staff over the coming days."

He shrugged. "No problem."

"HE'S SURROUNDED BY A FEW PEOPLE." Dewi opened the car door for her.

"I know and, unfortunately, we are going to have to interview the lot."

"I take it you don't suspect the house staff of bombing the place?"

"I don't see why they would be involved, though we can't rule anyone out at this stage. However, house staff can be very good at picking up gossip. If anyone close to Rothwell bears a serious grudge against him, they will most likely know who."

As the DS fired up the engine, Yvonne's eyes wandered once more over the crime scene. In her mind's eye, Ted still lay where he had fallen, and would continue to do so until the case was solved. She thought of the van driver, whose body she had not seen because of the chaotic mess that was the vehicle's leftovers. If the man was innocent, he deserved justice. His family would be as devastated as Ted's.

"Is that the NCA?" she asked, referring to the National Crime Agency as she pointed to two men walking around the grounds.

"Looks like it." Dewi slowed the car. "Do you want to speak to them?"

She observed the officers in the NCA's shiny black jackets with white crowns on the back. They were deep in conversation with SOCO. "No, they look busy enough. We can catch up with them later."

"Are you worried they'll hound us off of the case?" Dewi grinned.

"Perhaps..." She turned back to her sergeant. "But, if they do, it will be because they believe organised crime is involved. In which case, we should draw on their expertise. I will talk to them at some point. If serious gangs have infiltrated our patch, I want to know about it."

"Could be Albanians." Dewi grimaced.

"That is what I was thinking..." She nodded. "But if it was a serious crime gang, they would have made sure Rothwell was home and either abducted him or extorted money some other way, wouldn't they? According to the singer, no-one has contacted him at all. If he is telling us the truth, the bombing may be a scare tactic. To a gang, the van driver and security guard would simply have been collateral damage."

"By the time we get back, Callum and Dai should have the name of the driver and the company he worked for."

"I hope so. I want to speak to that company as soon as possible."

YVONNE SCANNED Callum's notes for the Riverdale bombing.

The deceased driver of the van was forty-one-year-old Martin Hawes, working for a company called Headwind Couriers. They were head-quartered in Shrewsbury, covering large swathes of England and Wales.

Headwind Couriers had sent their deputy manager, Daniel Smith or Danny, to speak with the murder investigation team. They were then to visit the scene where Martin was killed and lay a wreath left on behalf of the company.

She spotted him as soon as she reached the bottom of the station stairs. A broad gentleman, he was standing at the front desk in a dark blue pin-striped suit, hand-combing what meagre hair he possessed. He took out a handkerchief to mop his red face.

"Mr Daniel Smith?" she asked, her head cocked to see his eyes.

"Yes, that's me." He walked towards her, a musky damp heat emanating from him.

"Come through to the interview room," she said, showing the direction he should follow. "We have air-conditioning in there."

"Thank goodness." His smile was a bared-toothed grimace. There was a tension in his muscles as he walked in front of her.

She poured water from a jug on the table while he took his jacket off, placing it in front of him as he hung the coat on the back of his chair.

"Thank you." He gulped down several mouthfuls before rolling up his shirtsleeves; gazing at her expectantly.

"Thank you for coming to see us today. I should imagine it has been a fraught time for you at the office."

He puffed his cheeks out, blowing air through pursed lips. "You can say that again. Everyone at the company is in shock. Martin's death was a horrible blow to all of us. The drivers are on edge and demanding extra security measures. There's also talk that Martin's family intend on suing us for negligence."

"Really?" Yvonne tilted her head. "Why?"

"They think we are not taking driver safety and security seriously enough. There have been accusations in the local press about us putting profits before staff, and caring more about delivery times than their safety."

"And what are you thinking?" The DI's voice was soft as she scoured his face.

"I believe we do what we can with what we have."

"Meaning?"

"Meaning we take all reasonable precautions, but you

can't cover every eventuality. I mean, this sort of thing is so rare. The sorting staff are trained for what to do if they think a package is suspicious. And we have a sniffer dog at our main depot. We call the police with any concerns but, like I say, the incidents are rare, and we have never had a package explode like that before. To be honest, no-one has even confirmed with us whether it was one of our packages. As far as we know at the moment, the device could have come from anywhere. We cannot confirm how it got into the van until we know more about the bomb and what it was contained in. I was actually hoping you might know more?" He raised his brows at Yvonne.

She sighed. "I'm afraid I know little more about the package than you do. I understand it is still under investigation by specialist forensic officers, and the NCA may take the lead on the investigation. At first glance, it looks to be an improvised device. I cannot tell you any more than that, I'm afraid."

"Can't, or won't?" He frowned, his tone hostile.

"You seem annoyed."

"I was hoping to take something back to the office. It feels like the police are deliberately keeping tight-lipped, like there is a cover-up going on."

"Not from where I stand." Yvonne leaned back in her chair. "We can't tell you what we don't know. However, I can say that this is an ongoing, active investigation, so we are unlikely to tell the public everything we learn straight away. Some things should be withheld in order to ensure a conviction when we catch the perpetrator or perpetrators. Surely, you understand that? It is much too early to say anything about the device at the moment."

He took a plastic file from his briefcase case. "You asked

for paperwork for the delivery to Riverdale Mansion. I brought everything we had with me."

"Great." She leaned in, taking the file from his hands and opening the clip.

"It's a copy of the delivery schedule, and the basic details of the three parcels due to be delivered to the mansion on that day."

"Hmm..." She perused the meagre lines. "Three packages, one of which was heavy enough to require two people to carry it."

"That is correct."

"It's listed as being from Sentry Furnishings. Have you spoken to them?"

"We tried the mobile number given. It doesn't work. And it appears from our research there is no such company."

"What about the other two parcels? Both say here they were from a florist?"

"They check out... Those packages were addressed to a Peter Davies. That's all I know."

The DI recognised the addressee — Pete, the surviving security guard. She pursed her lips. "How long do you keep your records?"

He frowned in concentration. "Six years? I think I'm right in saying? I have that timeframe in my head, anyway."

"So you could tell us how regularly your company took parcels to Riverdale, and the names of the addressees?"

"We could get our admins onto it, yes."

"How long until we can have that information?"

"We could have it with you inside of a week?"

"That would be good. Faster, if you can?"

"I'll get onto it as soon as I get back. I have a wreath in the car, I have to lay it near the mansion gates, and photograph it in place before I get back."

"For Martin's family?"

"For our staff... We are releasing Martin's pension for his wife and kids. Helen is distraught, as you can imagine."

"How old are the children?"

"He left behind a boy and a girl, seventeen and twenty-one, respectively."

"So young..." She sighed. "Such a shame..."

"Yes, and the son lives at home with mum, so the sooner his benefits are released, the better."

"Is Martin's wife the complainant intending to sue?"

He nodded. "She and his parents."

"I see."

"Obviously, we will give our security measures an overhaul, but it's hard to see how we could have prevented what happened. It's easy to judge with hindsight, but companies and recipients alike put pressure on us to deliver in the fastest time possible. People are increasingly impatient these days. We're damned if we do more checks, and damned if we don't."

"Was Martin depressed? Suicidal?"

"Not to our knowledge... He attended Alcoholics Anonymous for a while, according to our boss, but hadn't had a drink in eighteen months. Wait, you don't think he might have done this himself, do you?"

"Did you know Martin personally?"

He shook his head. "To be honest, I don't even know if I would have recognised him by sight. We have seven depots spread around the country. I am based at our headquarters in Birmingham. Martin was based in our Ludlow depot. I saw the photograph in his employee file, and the one shown on the news. I think that was probably the first time I laid eyes on him." He checked his watch. "Will there be much more? I really ought to be going. I said I would be back at the office by four and it is mid-day already."

"Of course..." She rose from her chair. "I'll see you out, but we will be in touch again if we believe your company can help us further."

"Understood."

DAI GREETED her back in the office. He and Callum had been reading through Martin Hawes' Social Media, and talking with those friends and family who had come forward via telephone. "Ma'am, apparently Martin had only been with Headwind Couriers for six months."

"Really? Did they say what he was doing prior to that?"

"He was an electrician by training. Completed an apprenticeship ten years ago. He worked for a few small firms before deciding that the long hours and winter call-outs were not for him. That's when he applied to Headwind."

"How long ago was the company established? Do we know? I should have asked their deputy manager, but it slipped my mind."

Dai checked his notes. "It says here it was a start-up in two-thousand-fourteen. It's been going for nine years."

"Wow..." She whistled. "They expanded fast. Daniel Smith told me they have seven depots already. They are evidently doing a lot of business. He said they have been under a great deal of pressure."

Dai nodded. "More and more people buy goods online these days. I'm not surprised."

"Did you find anything in Martin's social media showing depressive tendencies or suicidal ideation?"

The DC shook his head. "Nothing. There were a couple of posts suggesting he or someone he knew had struggled with alcohol use."

"He had been going to Alcoholics Anonymous." She tilted her head. "Could you dig into that a little further? Find out if he ever expressed suicidal thoughts."

"Sure, no problem."

"How are his friends and family?"

"Well, they are obviously grieving, and in shock, but they seem sure the bomb would have been nothing to do with Martin. His sister said he wasn't one for picking fights. And he has never mentioned wanting to blow anything up or using extreme measures to seek revenge."

"Have we had word yet on the device?"

Dai shook his head. "Not yet, but we're expecting a briefing in the next twenty-four hours."

"Headwind's paperwork confirmed there were three parcels, one large and two small. The smaller ones were destined for Peter Davies, the surviving security guard. They were from a florist. I want to ask Peter about the smaller packages. I'd like you to look at his social media. Maybe he had a wedding anniversary or his wife's birthday, but I think we should talk to him about them. He didn't tell myself or Dewi that he had been expecting packages the day of the bombing. He left out that important detail. I would like to know why he didn't tell us."

Dai made notes in his pocketbook. "I'll get that checked out this afternoon. We'll be digging into Rothwell's band and entourage as well, see if anything stands out."

"Good." She nodded. "They are certainly an interesting bunch. There's an ex-boyfriend in the background too. Rothwell's girlfriend, Jeanie, mentioned him. He made threats against Rothwell when the singer and Jeanie first got together. Although he appears to have moved on, I think we should look at him. I'll speak to Llewelyn. We'll need extra resources and maybe some extra bodies to help us sift through these characters."

"Oh, I almost forgot." Dai ran a hand through his hair. "NCA will pay us a visit tomorrow."

"The National Crime Agency?"

"Yes, they're taking the lead on the case until they know for certain whether organised crime is involved. They say they have no specific intel, but two of their officers will be with us tomorrow to brief and be briefed. They'll be talking to the Home Secretary the following day."

The DI pursed her lips while she thought about it. "Fine, we'll get everyone together before they arrive. It will be useful to have the NCA's input. They will probably have information on organised crime in our area that we do not have. It will be good to pick their brains." She grinned, winking at Dai. "Llewelyn will be shining his buttons tonight, eh?"

Dai laughed. "Guaranteed, he'll be here in full uniform before anyone else has properly woken up."

3

THE SERIOUS SQUAD

The following morning, as everyone gathered for the briefing, Yvonne approached the two men from the NCA. They were helping themselves to coffee at the back of the room, where Llewelyn had temporarily left them. "Yvonne Giles, pleased to meet you." She held out her hand.

The taller of the two men cocked his head. Appearing to be in his mid-forties; his eyes twinkled as he shook her hand. He was a good foot taller than she, with a full head of cropped copper-brown hair and a strong jawline. Both men were smart, wearing a shirt and a tie. "Geoff Taylor... You must be the DI that Chris was telling us about this morning? We understand you're the lead investigator?"

"Dave Hanlon," the smaller of the two men offered his hand. His smile was warm enough, but she could tell there was a good deal going on behind the eyes. He was around the same height as she. Yvonne didn't need to crick her neck to talk to him. His greying hair needed a trim, but the rest of him was dapper.

Despite the grey, she judged Hanlon to be a good five or

six years younger than Taylor. She smiled at them both. "Yes, I am the lead on the case. I understand you are NCA?"

"We are," Hanlon nodded. "I'm an officer, and Geoff is an investigator."

"Sorry to show my ignorance, but what's the difference?" she asked, aware that she should probably know this. However, as law enforcement agencies were constantly developing, so too was their jargon. It was difficult keeping up.

"About three grand." Taylor laughed.

"He's a bugger." Hanlon grinned. "Think of it as our equivalent of CID versus uniform, and you won't go far wrong." He flicked his head towards Taylor. "He's triple-warranted, with the powers of police, customs, and immigration. But don't courtesy, it'll go to his head."

"Got it." She laughed out loud. The DI couldn't help but take to them. She was about to call Dewi over, but DCI Chris Llewelyn interrupted, clearing his throat at the front of the room to gain everyone's attention.

The chatter died away.

"Good morning, everyone. I wanted to take this opportunity to introduce Geoff Taylor and Dave Hanlon." He pointed to the men standing next to the DI. "These officers from the NCA will liaise with us during this investigation. You'll probably see them around a fair bit. If you come across significant intel regarding the Riverdale bombing, these are the guys to talk to. And don't forget our own lead on the case, Yvonne."

He continued by outlining what they already knew about the incident, referring to images and schematics on the interactive board. When he had finished, he turned to face them all. "The perpetrators responsible for this bombing have already taken two lives. Our priority now is to find them and prevent it from happening again. If there are no further questions, I will hand you over to Geoff and Dave, who will brief you on local and national gang activity. Listen carefully, they are the things you will need to be aware of as you investigate this case."

"Thank you." Geoff loosened his tie and rolled up his shirt sleeves. "Let me start by saying we have no specific intel regarding this bombing. We hope to have the device identified and reconstructed within the next few days. That may help give us an idea of who made it. One of the dominant groups on our radar at the moment is the so-called Albanian mafia, who are involved in some seriously bad shit right now. They are closely involved with the Turkish and Italian mafias, most especially Ndrangheta of Calabria. The Ndrangheta control a massive share of the billion-dollar cocaine market in Europe. In fact, they are the number one distributors throughout the continent via the balkans, with a significant hub in London. These guys have their fingers in just about every criminal pie you can imagine. And they are not shy about using violence to get what they want; maiming or murdering anyone who stands in their way. They have a global reach, and are operative in not only in Europe, but in North- and South America, the Middle East, and Asia. In Albania, they have politicians on their payroll, and have infiltrated many of the country's institutions. That country is considered a narco-state." He wrote the main bullet points on the whiteboard before turning back to face them. "Like I say, we do not have specific intel linking them to this bombing, but it could be the prelude of extortion. They may contact Dean Rothwell, offering him protection from further bombings for money. Of course, they would simply be offering protection from themselves, but this is how they operate. If you find any connection to Albanian gangs, we would like to know immediately. Proceed with caution, and always wear your personal protective equipment. Like I said, they are not afraid to use violence, even with law enforcement. It's important you remember that. Any questions?"

Several hands raised around the room, and Geoff and Dave answered them one-by-one.

Yvonne crossed the floor to Dewi. "What do you think? Is it credible? Could this be what we're dealing with?"

He shrugged. "None of our informants have mentioned Albanian gang activity. I suppose it is a worthwhile line of enquiry, but I'm not convinced it is what we are looking at with the Riverdale bombing. But until we have other plausible motives, it's good to be aware of the possibilities, I guess."

"They seem a nice duo, Taylor and Hanlon. Even if this proves not to be the work of Albanian criminals, the NCA could help us."

"I best keep on the right side of them, then." Dewi grinned. "No jokes about them being FBI wannabes."

"Absolutely not." Yvonne pulled a face. "Don't you dare get me into trouble, Dewi Hughes."

He laughed at the mock-horror on her face. "Seriously though, those guys are civil servants. There's probably a lot they won't be able to tell us... Official Secrets Act, and all that."

She rubbed her chin. "I'm sure they'll give us relevant information if they have it. So..." She grinned. "Keep on their good side."

～

PETER DAVIES, the surviving security guard from the Riverdale bombing, had a noticeable middle-age spread. This was emphasised by the unfortunate positioning of a large belt-buckle dividing the hump into two. The man was around five-foot-eight, with a discernible wheeze to his breathing as he took a seat opposite.

As Yvonne and Dewi readied their paperwork, the DI noticed a fine sheen of sweat on the top of their interviewee's head, where his hair was sparse.

"Are you okay?" She asked, referring to his breath-lessness.

"Yeah, fine..." He plopped down on the chair. "I get hay fever, and I forgot my inhaler this morning. And that was after my wife reminded me to take it, as we have a pollen bomb over the UK this week according to the BBC weather forecast."

"Would you like us to send someone to the chemist? It's not far..."

He shook his head. "I'll be going home after this. I'll be okay until then."

"As you wish." Yvonne spread her notes in front of her. "How are you feeling now, Pete, after the shock of what happened?"

"Not too bad." He wrung his hands. "I've had some nightmares since that day, and I keep seeing... I keep seeing the van and the bodies. I wake up several times a night, and I'm under the doctor at the moment."

"I can imagine." She pressed her lips together.

"Still, I'm in better shape than Ted, eh?" He shook his head, lowering his eyes. "It was an awful way to die. I wouldn't wish that on my worst enemy."

"No..." Yvonne tilted her head, her voice soft; gaze

steady. "Pete, I understand two of the parcels being delivered that day were yours. Is that right?"

His eyes snapped to hers. "I think that's correct, yes."

"Were you expecting them?"

"I was, but it slipped my mind completely, given what happened that day."

"Is that why you didn't tell us about them when we spoke to you outside of Riverdale?"

"That would be why, yes." He shifted in his seat, loudly clearing phlegm from his throat.

The DI read her notes. "It says here there were two parcels destined for you from a florist in Shrewsbury. Is that right?"

"Yes."

"Would you usually take delivery of personal items at your employer's address?"

"Er, not normally... No."

"What was different about that day? Why were they delivered to Riverdale?"

"It was mine and the wife's twentieth wedding anniversary the following day. I could have had the stuff delivered to our home, but I knew my wife would open the boxes, and I wanted it to be a surprise."

"So, these were anniversary gifts?"

"Yes... There would have been flowers in one box, and chocolates and wine in the other."

"I see."

"Of all the excuses a man could use for not giving his wife an anniversary gift, mine has to be one of the most unbelievable. But there it was. It happened. Brenda's happy anniversary presents blown to smithereens in an instant."

Dewi pursed his lips. "And the fact you had parcels

onboard that van slipped your mind because of the explosion?"

"Yes, because my thoughts were focussed on Ted and the van driver. Two people were lying dead in the driveway. That kind of overrides everything else, doesn't it?"

"Did you wonder what had blown them up?"

"Well, yeah... Of course I did. But I was trying to process what had happened. You don't honestly think Brenda's flowers blew the van up, do you?" He raised both eyebrows.

"It wouldn't be our first thought, Peter, but we are still investigating the device, and how it got into that van."

"Well, Hanberry's Bouquets, that's the florist in Shrewsbury, have been my go-to place for years. I have used them many times before. Never once have their deliveries ever blown up." He folded his arms. "I think you can rule them out as being the culprits."

"Why did you delay the shift handover with Ted?"

"I told you, I needed a leak. I was desperate and had to go pee before my shift started. It wouldn't be the first time the changeover was delayed."

"Why didn't you go to the toilet earlier to ensure you could do the handover on time?"

Pete leaned back in his chair, arms still crossed on his chest. "Oh, I see... I delayed the handover because I knew there was a bomb being delivered, and I didn't want to get caught up in it. Is that where this is going? My mate died in that explosion, and you think I might have had something to do with it? You people are unbelievable."

"We are not assuming anything." Yvonne kept her voice low and steady. "We understand things by asking questions. You want us to do a thorough job, right? You want Ted's killers punished, don't you?"

"Of course I do, but you need to be out there banging on

doors, not in here quizzing me. I am a victim of this too, you know?"

"We understand that, Pete. To reassure you, we will investigate the origin of every parcel on that vehicle."

"Fine." He sighed, unfolding his arms.

"Do you know anything about Sentry Furnishings?"

"Sentry Furnishings?" He frowned.

"Yes... Apparently, there was a large parcel listed as a two-man carry from that company which, as far as we know, doesn't exist."

"Never heard of it." He scratched his head, still frowning. "Nope, not come across any place by that name. And it's been quite some time since I bought furniture."

"Do you know if Rothwell ordered furniture? Had he instructed you guys to take a delivery?"

"I don't recall him asking me. I think you should ask him about that yourself."

"We did."

"I guess he might have told Ted about a delivery that day, but no-one mentioned anything to me."

"You would tell us if they did?"

"Of course, I would."

"Very well."

"You don't think Rothwell would have bombed his own place, do you? That is crazy."

"We are keeping an open mind. We are not assuming or ruling anything out."

"Hmm..." He fell quiet.

"Do you get on well with your employer?"

"We have a reasonable professional relationship. I have very little to complain about. I mean, he is sometimes late arriving back from tour. He is not always there when he says he will be. And he rings up now and then to ask us to do other jobs for him. Things not related to our key roles as security guards, but that's just him. We got used to it over the years."

"What sort of things does he ask you to do? What do you consider beyond your role?"

"He occasionally rings up to ask us to look for things, or to clear out stuff out for him."

"What sort of stuff?"

"Rubbish, mostly... Things he doesn't have use for anymore. One time, he rang up to say he and his mates had left the place in a mess and the cleaner had phoned in sick for the week. He wanted us to sort out the chaos."

"And did you?"

"Of course, he pays our wages."

"Surely, you have a contract agreeing your pay and conditions?"

"We do, but he could still sack us if he wanted to. Rothwell can be impulsive, especially when he is on something."

"On something?" Yvonne narrowed her eyes.

Pete's face reddened. "Yeah, you know, he sometimes has a bit too much to drink."

"You said, 'on something'. That implies a substance other than alcohol."

"Yeah, well, he's rocker, isn't he? They aren't shrinking violets, are they? They use all sorts."

"Do you know he uses drugs? Do you have definitive proof? Have you witnessed him taking anything?"

"I've seen him smoking dope, and Ted told me the guests were snorting stuff at parties."

"Ted isn't here to confirm that. Did you not work while parties were going on?"

"I did, but I never had cause to walk into the main hall when they were all in there. They could be really loud."

"Why did Ted go in there?"

"It was usual to let them know we were knocking off. We only work nights when Rothwell is away. When he and his friends are home, we leave them at it after six o'clock. We man the gates and check in deliveries and services during the day when he is home, and leave him to it at night. It's different when the band is on tour. We can't leave the house with no-one watching it. Rothwell has had one or two break-ins in the past."

"Really? When did they happen?"

"Oh, we're talking a few years ago, but it is why he increased our hours to ensure it didn't happen again."

"I see..."

"He had a load of expensive jewellery taken during one burglary."

"Really?"

"The gang had been watching his house, and knew when he was coming and going. They knew his tour dates, and had worked out which rooms were likely to hold the expensive belongings. They caused a lot of damage, too. He's had increased security ever since."

"Have you observed anyone hanging around the house in recent weeks?"

"Not anyone persistent..."

"So, you have seen someone?"

"We see a fair few people coming and going. He's a celebrity. Fans sometimes rock up to look at where he lives, and see if they can get a glance of him or the band. That's par for the course for any rock star. We never let them get too close, but we don't stop them from looking from beyond the gates. It's something fans sometimes like to do. Rothwell considered introducing paid fan tours before his house was ransacked. The break-ins put him off."

"I see."

"We were glad. They would have been a nightmare for us to supervise."

"He would have taken on more staff, surely?"

Davies grimaced. "He can be tight-fisted with paying staff. He gives as little as he can get away with. If we had asked him to take on extra security for the tours, he would almost certainly have said no. In fact, he would probably have had a heart attack right there and then."

"Even after the break-ins?"

"Even after the break-ins. He already had two security staff. He would have wanted Ted and I to cover everything."

"Does he pay you overtime?"

"He pays for any extra hours in the week at the normal hourly rate. If we do extra on weekends, he pays time and a half. I told you, he is tight with his money."

"Does it make you resent him?"

"Not enough to blow his house up, if that is where you are heading with this?" He frowned. "And Ted would never have done something like that. He was a thoroughly decent bloke."

"Do you know anyone who might have wanted to harm Rothwell? Or damage his property? Scare him?"

He shook his head. "No-one I can think of."

"Had he fallen out with anyone recently? Maybe had a heated argument?"

"Well, he can be hot-headed sometimes. I mean, he has calmed down a lot compared to when he was younger, but he isn't shy when speaking his mind, if someone has annoyed him. I think the courts fined him for road rage a while ago."

"Road rage?"

"Yeah, he had a right go at some poor woman at traffic

lights in Shrewsbury a year or two back. Nothing physical, just gave her a load of verbals, but they weren't words you would use in polite company. Put it that way."

"What do his friends think of that?"

"They're used to him. They laugh, and call it artistic temperament, and say it's all part of being in show biz. I think it's downright rude, personally."

"Could Rothwell have done this to himself?"

"I don't see why he would. I know he can act a little crazy, but I don't know why he would want to damage his own property. Unless..."

"Unless what?"

"Unless the package was supposed to blow up the house and cause extensive damage. Perhaps he might do something like that for the insurance money? But I doubt it. He loves that mansion. And I am not aware of him having money issues. But you'd have to ask him that."

She nodded. "What did Ted like to do in his spare time?"

"Ted? He liked to fish. He would spend hours on the banks of the River Severn, or the Fachwen Pool, on a Saturday. And, when his brother was down for a visit, they would sometimes play a round of golf at the St. Giles club in Newtown. That was how he unwound. His wife, Rhonda, is a member of the local Knit and Natter Club, and she sometimes helps with the Newtown Round Table functions and fundraising. They were the sort of couple who didn't feel the need to live in each other's pockets, though no-one could doubt the strength of the love they had for each other. I expect Rhonda is feeling lost." He bowed his head.

"Have you thought about visiting her? Paying your respects? It might help."

He sighed. "I've thought about it, but I wanted to give her time to grieve in peace. I should think her close friends and family have been going to see her, and I wouldn't want to intrude. But, when the time is right, I will go to see her; tell her it was an honour to work with her husband."

"I am sure she would like that."

"I ought to be going." Pete checked his watch. "I am expected back at work in an hour. Rothwell said he is going to advertise Ted's job but, until then, there is only me to keep things going."

"Well, you take it steady." Yvonne rose from her seat. "DS Hughes will see you out."

4

A CASE OF SELF HARM?

"Your phone is ringing." Dai pushed his pen behind his ear and picked up Yvonne's mobile from her desk. He ran with it to where she and Dewi were going over the details in the Riverdale bombing case.

"Thank you, Dai." She accepted the phone, frowning in concentration as she strained to hear the speaker on the other end.

"It's Geoff," the voice said. "Geoff Taylor from the NCA." He sounded out of breath and, judging by the traffic in the background, was near a road.

"Hey, Geoff..." She smiled into the phone. "How's it going?"

"It's going okay, thanks. Listen, we are still investigating the device that blew up the van at Rothwell's mansion."

"Okay..."

"We haven't ruled out organised crime, but I thought you should know that it's looking unlikely. From what we have seen so far, we think it was a fairly crude device; likely home-made, and without the sophistication, we normally associate with hardened professionals. If this was done by a gang, they didn't want it to look like it was. It matches nothing made by known organisations. I can't go into specifics, I'm afraid, but I would advise you to look out for evidence that someone has been researching how to make explosive devices."

"You mean Google searches, that sort of thing?"

"Google, the local libraries, maybe even second-hand purchases of books from the internet, that sort of thing. If you are going into a suspect's house, they may have books lying around. Look for notepaper stuffed in relevant pages, perhaps with drawings on. We think your bomber is likely inexperienced, so they will have looked up how to make the mechanism, probably recently. It matches nothing from known bombers or gang members. We can often identify the maker from the way they put the thing together and the components they used. The Riverdale apparatus was fairly crude, but the bomber took care with it. They will have made notes and drawings which you might find if they haven't destroyed them already."

"Knowing our luck, they will have burned them." The DI grimaced.

"Perhaps, but I doubt it. I think they will have kept them, especially if they want to try again. The trouble they took to do this, and the time invested, suggests intention for ongoing use."

"That is really helpful, thank you." Yvonne pondered Taylor's words, ruminating on the chances the bomber could try again. If the original aim had been to damage or destroy Rothwell's house, or harm him personally, that goal had not yet been achieved.

He continued. "Like I say, we haven't ruled out organised crime completely. This could be a new group on the patch, maybe from Eastern Europe or the Middle East, but we increasingly think this unlikely. I will keep you informed where I can, Yvonne."

"Thank you, Geoff, I appreciate it. Take Care."

"NCA?" Dewi asked.

Yvonne nodded. "That was Geoff Taylor. They think our bomber is self-taught, and not a professional criminal."

"Are they packing up and bowing out?"

"No, they are still looking into this, but Taylor thinks it unlikely organised crime is involved. He said to look for signs a suspect has been researching the making of explosives on the internet, or using how-to books. They believe the bomber will have made extensive notes and drawings, and is likely to try again."

"Rothwell has a library at the house, doesn't he? I saw it when we were there the other day. It must have two or three thousand books, at least."

She rubbed her chin. "Perhaps we ought to look there. Even if the perp researched this on the internet, they are likely to have kept notes somewhere. If the singer did this to himself, the drawings may be in his library. It's a long-shot, perhaps, but I wanted to speak to him again, anyway." She turned her attention to Dai and Callum. "Could you guys dig into Rothwell's finances for me? Apparently, he doesn't pay out more than he has to for his employees. He could simply be cautious with his finances, but is this the explanation? Or has he got money worries? Enormous debts? Bank loans? Does he owe money to loan sharks? Does he spend more on leisure than he does on his staff? It's possible he orchestrated this tragedy for a claim on his insurance. Or maybe he borrowed money from nasty characters and didn't pay them back. The explosion could have been their version of punishment."

Callum looked up from his computer. "No problem... When are you going to see him?"

She checked her watch. "Later this afternoon, around three-ish."

"Right, I'll make a start and see what I can dig up before you go. If he's dodgy, you don't want to give the man wriggle room."

Yvonne and Dewi parked in front of the thirty-six roomed Riverdale mansion, Rothwell's Georgian home.

Built in seventeen-seventy-three, the house was almost three-hundred-years-old and showing advanced age. The sandstone had discoloured to a muddy-brown; its brickwork eroded by centuries of wind and rain.

The grand entrance porch, supported by two giant Corinthian pillars, led into the tall-ceilinged grand hallway; a carved mahogany staircase split into two, following along walls adorned with both modern and antique art. The DI wasn't an aficionado, but to her mind, several of the pieces clashed wildly with each other. Modern art juxtaposed old masters. Something told her Rothwell had been the architect behind their placements.

The walls, painted in a rich terracotta, showed signs of water damage in places. Salt stains and traces of mould could be seen where blemishes had been crudely wiped away. Against the rich wall-colour, several white pillars, marbled with yellow and grey, stood out. The whole was an ostentatious, if tainted, room designed to impress.

Dean Rothwell came through a door to their right. "Aha, you're here. We're in the sitting room. I've asked the housekeeper to make us some tea. I could do with something stronger, but tea will have to do."

They followed him to where the rest of his entourage sat lounging and chatting. Simes had his feet on the table, ankles crossed, when they entered. The rest looked up nervously from their chatter, unsure why the detectives had returned.

"Hey everyone, you remember DI Giles and DS Hughes? They are back to have another talk with us about the bombing." He gave the officers a sideways glance. "Because apparently they didn't get enough when they came the last time."

Ignoring the dig, Yvonne pressed her lips together, her eyes passing over each of their faces.

Andy, Trev, Dave, Simes, Jeanette, and Patti all looked at Rothwell expectantly. It was obvious they expected him to be the spokesperson.

"So how can we help you this time, officers?" he asked.

"This is a beautiful home." Yvonne looked directly at him.

"Thank you." He narrowed his eyes. "But I'm sure you didn't come here to tell me that."

"You are right, of course. We didn't come here to admire your home."

"Then why did you come? I thought we'd told you all we could about the tragic events outside. We can't tell you anymore because we weren't here when it happened."

"I understand what you're saying, but we have further questions." Yvonne took out her notebook. "Would you like to talk to us on your own?" she asked.

He shrugged. "I am not worried about talking in front of my friends. I don't mind them hearing anything I have to say."

"I wanted to ask you about a road rage incident that occurred some years ago."

"What road rage incident?" He frowned. "I don't know what you're talking about."

"You rowed a woman at traffic lights, and were subsequently found guilty of section five public order and given a fine." The DI scoured his face.

"Oh, that... Why is that even relevant?"

"Would you say you have a temper?"

"If someone upsets me, yes, I do. Who doesn't if they feel they have been treated unfairly?"

"Did you think the victim had been unfair?"

"She cut me up on a roundabout. She wasn't looking where she was going. I caught up with her when she stopped at the lights and gave her a piece of my mind. It could have been a nasty accident."

Jeanette and Patti exchanged glances.

Trev got up, crossed to a drinks cabinet disguised as an enormous globe, and poured himself a large scotch.

"Why did they charge you with public order?"

"I swore at her... several times. Other drivers saw me and called the police."

"You must have caused quite a stir."

He shrugged. "I suppose I did. I was tired and strung out, so I let the lady have it. Of course I felt bad afterwards, but it was too late by then, wasn't it? I couldn't take it back."

"Was that before or after you were fined?"

"The magistrates reminded me I was a public figure and had a duty to set a good example for others. I mean, I wasn't the first rock star to misbehave, and I won't be the last. It's almost expected of us. And, if you must know, I felt bad straight after the incident. I acted in haste and temper, and I regretted it."

"Would you describe yourself as vengeful?"

He gritted his teeth. "Oh, I get it. You think I master-minded the bomb to get back at someone? Who would I be looking to get revenge on? I am surrounded by friends and confidants. Why would I wish to harm any of them? What do you take me for?"

The DI nodded. "I understand. I ask these questions to be thorough. It's part of my job."

He folded his arms. "Fine."

She glanced at her notes. "Forensics have said the bomb was crudely made. They don't believe it was built by an expert. They think it is likely the perpetrator looked up methods of bomb-making on the internet. Do you know anyone who might have done that? Has anyone mentioned reading about this sort of thing to you?"

He looked around at his friends. "No-one has said anything to me. Has anyone mentioned something like this to any of you?"

The friends shook their heads. "Jeanette looked at her watch, her face sullen."

He turned back to the detectives. "You see? We know nothing. We are the victims here. You should be out there, poking around in other people's business instead of ours."

"Do you have a toilet?" Yvonne put her notebook back in her bag.

"Do you need one?" Rothwell raised both brows.

She grimaced. "I'm afraid I do. It's been a while since I was in the office."

"Fine." He sighed. "It's down the corridor, third door on you right, immediately before you get to the back stairwell."

"Thank you."

As Dewi asked a general question about the house, the DI set off down the corridor. The DS had told her that the entrance to the library was at the end of the corridor, near the back stairwell. She ran light-footed to the door and pushed it open.

The double-aspect room was well lit from four large sash windows which ran almost floor to ceiling. The two remaining walls, on her left and right as she entered, contained alcove bookshelves with oak panelling at their base. Yvonne suspected the books numbered in their thousands. Many of them appeared well-worn.

Within the room were four round tables and carved oak chairs, where someone could sit and read. Beneath each of the large windows was a built-in seat with scatter cushions. No books had been left out of the shelves, and there was no loose paper anywhere.

The DI crossed to the shelving to her left, to see if any of the books stuck out a little, evidence someone might have read them recently. All were perfectly in place. Her eyes flicked over the spines.

"I thought you needed the toilet?" Rothwell's tone was accusatory as he stood in the doorway, hands on hips, expanded pupils rendering his eyes black.

The DI jumped, heart pumping hard in her chest. "I love books," she blurted. "I noticed you had a library the last time I came, and I couldn't resist taking a peek. Forgive me, I have loved old books since I was a child. I love the smell and feel of them."

"You weren't thinking of stealing any, were you?"

"No, of course I wasn't." The DI did her best to look imperious. "The door was ajar, and I simply had to have a quick look. I should have asked first... I'm sorry."

"Well, you missed the toilet by a few feet."

"I'll head there now. I really do need to go."

He held the door open, his arm up high, forcing her to duck underneath.

She hated being on the back foot. The DI mentally chastised herself for not having closed the library door. But how was she to know he would follow her?

Once satisfied she really was intending using the lavatory, Rothwell left her alone and returned to the sitting room.

Yvonne closed the toilet door and leaned against it, allowing her heart time to calm down. Should snooping be required in the future, she would be extra cautious. Dean Rothwell was clearly a man with a low flash-point and had little trust in others. What exactly was he frightened of?

5

TASHA'S TAKE

Two days later, the emergency services were called to the magistrates' court in Welshpool. A courier wearing a motorcycle helmet had left a package, inside of which was a ticking timer and wiring linked to a wrapped oblong object. Even to the untrained eye of the lady who opened it, it was obviously a bomb. Her scream as she let go of the package startled both admin and security staff alike. She threw it into the street, where it still lay crumpled and silent.

Yvonne and Dewi were told to remain beyond the cordon as a bomb disposal team readied to examine the package with a remote-controlled robotic arm. They had parked their lorry on the opposite end of the street. It sported the blue-edged yellow stripe of the Army Logistics Corps. They had cleared the road of people and evacuated the court and surrounding buildings comprising shops and flats.

Reporters jostled for position at the front of the gathering crowd, pushing a microphone in front of anyone who came near them. Uniformed police reprimanded photographers many times for transgressing the cordon.

There was near silence in the street as the wheeled robot approached the package.

Yvonne flicked her eyes to the truck, where a young man had donned heavy-duty protective gear and helmet. In his kit, he appeared larger than life, like an astronaut treading the moon, though his suit was dark green, and sported a massive neck guard. The scene looked like something from the movie The Hurt Locker.

As the robot explored the parcel, the suited man safely viewed its contents remotely via an iPad screen fed from a camera on the roving arm.

Perspiration beaded on Dewi's upper lip. He leaned in towards the DI. "I don't envy him his job," he said, eyes glued to the robot as it approached the device.

"He's a brave man." She nodded. "I hope they can successfully diffuse it without a controlled explosion. We need to know how it's put together."

Dewi scratched his cheek. "Do you think it's the same bomber?"

"I think it likely, don't you? What are the chances of two bombers working within thirty miles of each other and both delivering boxed packages?"

"Could be terrorists." Dewi nodded, pulling a face. "But I really hope not."

"Perhaps, although they would usually have claimed responsibility by now. Over a week has passed since the Riverdale explosion, and no-one has owned up. There have been no demands, and no-one is boasting. This feels more like an individual pursuing a vendetta, to me."

"Hey up, it looks like the boy is going in." Dewi squinted as he watched the soldier slowly approach the package.

"They call this the long walk..." He ran his tongue over his upper lip. "Once he gets up close, his gear can no longer protect him if the thing goes off."

Yvonne raised a brow. "Thanks, Dewi. You're making me feel so much better."

"Sorry..." He grimaced. "It's the nerves."

She didn't envy the soldier as he knelt in front of the device in the full heat of the day, gently peeling back the cardboard to peer inside.

The DI swallowed hard.

Dewi cleared his throat.

Finally, the soldier stood and waved an arm at his colleagues.

"Has he diffused it?" Yvonne craned her neck, trying to see.

"I guess he must have." Dewi shrugged.

"Come on." Yvonne headed toward the nearest beat officer, who was busy ensuring no-one from the crowd crossed the cordon. "Let's ask if we can talk to the soldiers."

"Right-oh." He followed her as she flashed her badge at the constable.

The officer held up his hand, about to ask them to stay back, when the suited disposal guy took his helmet off.

"See?" Yvonne pointed to the soldier. "He's taken his mask off. It's all over."

"Fine." The constable stepped back, lifting the tape for them to go underneath.

They waited for the soldier to finish relaying his findings to his colleagues in the truck.

Finally, he turned, raising his eyebrows when he saw Yvonne.

"DI Giles," she held up her badge. "I'm an officer with Dyfed-Powys police."

"Sergeant Denholm." He gave them a brusque nod.

"Can you tell us what you found? I know we'll get the information eventually, but we were hoping you could give us a heads-up?"

He checked his watch, showing his time was precious. "Whoever constructed that bomb didn't wire it securely. The live had detached, probably shaken loose when it was tossed into the street. It wouldn't have exploded."

"Really?"

"If it had gone off, it would have badly injured or killed the poor sod who opened the package." He pulled a face. "I could see the live wire hanging loose when I viewed it through the rover's camera. Once I got up close and personal, I confirmed it wasn't viable. You should go back beyond the cordon, as we may need to do a controlled explosion. It's not safe until we have contained the explosive material."

"Understood, thank you."

He continued. "Everything in the package, and the way it was put together, has been recorded via our camera. Forensics will take care of the rest. We are in charge of the device until it's made completely safe."

"Thank you, Sergeant."

Yvonne and Dewi headed back the way they had come, leaving the Logistics Corps to their work.

"Well, this opens up a whole new can of worms." The DS grimaced. "Somebody is not a happy bunny."

The DI pressed her lips together. "When we get back, can you find out who was due to appear in the court today? And what the charges were?"

"No problem. I'll request a copy of the court list."

"Thank you."

"Do you want the names of the magistrates presiding, too?"

"Please."

THE SEA ROLLED GENTLY over colourful stones, continuing centuries of rounding and polishing. Whooshing up the beach, it fell back with a rattle as it sucked at tiny pebbles and filled the air with that distinctive salty fish odour of the ocean.

The effect calmed Yvonne from the inside out. It had been a while since she had felt this relaxed. She walked along the beach with Tasha, barefoot in a pale blue flowery dress; barely a cloud in the azure sky on a warm Saturday in Aberystwyth, on the West-Wales coast.

Tasha, also barefoot, carried their sandals; white linen trousers rolled up to her knees; sun glinting off chocolate hair.

"Could a day be more perfect?" The DI squinted as she faced her partner, putting a hand up to shield her eyes from the strong summer sun.

Tasha shook her head. "Definitely not... I wish time would slow so the day could last longer."

"Me too." Yvonne turned back to the sea, watching reflected light dancing on its surface. "We should do this more often, shouldn't we?"

Tasha grimaced. "If only work didn't get in the way."

"Do you have to leave again soon?" The DI tilted her head, a wistful expression on her face.

Tasha noticed light freckles coming out across her partner's nose as it reddened in the sun. "Middle of next week...

But it should only be for a few days this time. I hope to be back by Sunday."

"Shall we say we might come again on Sunday, then?"

"We *will* come again on Sunday." The psychologist jutted out her jaw. "Absolutely."

Yvonne lowered her eyes, watching their toes sinking into soft sand.

"Is something the matter?" Tasha asked, her voice gentle.

"I may have to work."

"Next Sunday?"

"I hope not but, yes, next weekend. You know we had a van explosion last week?"

"Yes…"

"Well, there was another package at the magistrate's court."

"Really?" Tasha frowned. "Oh, no…"

"It didn't go off, thankfully. Some wires had shaken loose, but it could have been really serious."

"Please be careful, Yvonne." Tasha placed a hand on her partner's arm. "I couldn't bear it if anything happened to you."

The DI pursed her lips. "I'm not worried for myself, but I am concerned about the people receiving these parcels. I hope there won't be any more, but I fear the worst."

"Any idea who is sending them?"

Yvonne shook her head. "We've been looking at the singer, Dean Rothwell and the people surrounding him, but after this latest attempt? It's beginning to look more like a disgruntled stranger having a pop at people or institutions they don't like. If the perpetrator is unrelated to the victims, they will be much harder to find and stop."

"Do you know where the packages were posted from?"

"My team is looking into it. The van was carrying a

parcel from a non-existent furniture company. We believe it was left at a village post office. Dai and Callum are trying to identify the person who took it there. The court package was left by a motorcycle courier. We need to identify him as soon as possible. CCTV captured the bike, but the licence plate was false, so not in any database. Whoever is doing this has really thought things through."

"What about the post office where the first package was left? Did it have CCTV? Have you got a decent look at the rider?"

The DI shook her head. "The post office was one of the few left which uses a mirror at the back to watch customers instead of a CCTV system. Like I said, this perp appears to have thought everything through. And we don't know whether he intends to strike again, or who the target might be if he does. The NCA and Counter-Terrorism are looking at the construction of the second device, but have so far stayed tight-lipped. The NCA told us that the first device, the one that went off, was of basic construction much like an amateur might do. They think the perp will have kept notes and schematics outlining how to make the device."

Tasha nodded. "That makes sense. It brings to my mind Ted Kaczynski, the so-called Unabomber. He terrorised the United States for a couple of decades until he was caught in nineteen-ninety-five."

"I've heard of him. He was a domestic terrorist, wasn't he?"

"Yeah, he was the university professor who took himself off into the wilderness to live. He wrote prolifically on what he saw as technology's destruction of the world, and people's way of life. If I remember rightly, he was a math-ematician. He blamed those who released modern tech for causing environmental damage. He was living a basic life in the Montana Mountains and sending homemade explosive devices through the post. It took two decades to catch him, beginning in nineteen-seventy-nine. He sent letters to news-papers demanding his personal manifesto be printed if they wanted the attacks to stop. I'm sorry to tell you this given your situation, but he killed three people, and injured over twenty during his campaign."

Yvonne ran a hand through her hair. "Oh, God... Let's hope we catch our bomber a lot faster than that."

"I have every faith in you, my love, but you had better keep yourself safe. I shall worry like crazy while I am in London, not being able to keep an eye on you."

"Are you ready for lunch?" The DI checked her watch. "I don't know about you, but I'm starving."

"Sure..." Tasha grinned. "But don't think I am letting you off from promising me you will do nothing dangerous."

"I promise I will exercise all caution." Yvonne smiled. "But only if I can eat within the next twenty minutes."

The psychologist laughed and set off running up the beach. "Come on then, move your backside, DI Giles."

THE DIMLY LIT alley was cloaked in secrecy as the moon's pale light struggled to penetrate a thick layer of darkness. The faint hum of distant traffic was drowned out by the silent anticipation hanging in the air. Two figures stood facing each other, identities veiled in shadow, as they exchanged a brief nod of recognition. It was a meeting orchestrated in whispers, a clandestine transaction where silence held sway over words.

An imposing figure, dressed in a tailored black suit, opened a small leather briefcase. It scratched on gravel as he placed it on the damp ground.

The second figure, attired in leather and a helmet as black as the surrounding darkness, bent to look at its contents.

In the ensuing stillness, a large sum of money changed hands, both parties aware of the high stakes involved. It was an evil dance of risk and reward. The suited man held his breath as the figure in the helmet counted the contents of the case. Stacks of crisp banknotes, meticulously arranged in neat rows, reflected in the meagre moonlight. The sheer volume of currency shimmered with an ethereal glow compared to the blackness around. The man in the helmet licked his lips.

The figures glanced at each other momentarily, their eyes meeting in that fleeting connection which conveyed so much with so little. No emotion on their faces; they were masters of concealment, adept at maintaining their respective facades. Their business was conducted in silence, an unspoken agreement to protect shared interests.

Gloved hands moved with calculated precision, closing the clasps of the case and lifting it from the ground.

Finally, as the encounter reached its conclusion, the figures faded into the night as effortlessly as they had arrived. The alley returned to its former quietude, undisturbed by the secrets to which it had borne witness.

6

THE MAN IN THE BLACK HELMET

When Yvonne arrived in the station on Monday morning, she found Dai and Callum already at their desks. "Wow, get you two..." She placed her linen jacket over the back of her chair. "Have you been home at all?"

Callum grinned. "Would you pay us more if we said no?"

She laughed. "You get more than enough overtime as it is. What have you got for me?"

Dai looked up from his screen. "The Sentry Furnishings package was taken into Tynderwen post office by a man wearing a black motorcycle helmet."

The DI crossed to her desk. "So, we are presumably looking at the same courier who delivered the package to the court?"

"It looks that way."

"Did you get any CCTV from elsewhere in the village? Ring doorbell footage? Anything to confirm the make of bike and which way the rider went? I'm loathe to call him the perpetrator, because we don't know the role he played.

He may simply have been a courier and not the person who made the bomb."

"Well, with your permission, I think we should get the local press to put out a description of the man in the black helmet and see if he comes forward."

"Absolutely..." She nodded. "Contact all local newspapers and Welsh news channels. Ask them to broadcast the description and anything else we know about him from the shop assistant and the staff at Welshpool court. If the motorcyclist is an innocent courier, he should contact us within a day or two."

"I'll get on it." Dai turned back to his computer.

Yvonne turned to Callum. "So Martin Hawes, the victim of the Riverdale bombing, picked up the package from Tynderwen post office. Is that right?"

"That is correct. The young woman, Helen Turpin, who worked that day, gave a description that matched Martin. She confirmed that Headwind Couriers was the company assigned to pick it up. It was a Headwind van parked outside when the package was removed. She said she had been exceptionally busy that morning with deliveries, so she didn't pay particular attention to the face of the guy who picked it up. She couldn't absolutely confirm it was Martin, but she had glanced out of the window and seen the Headwind van, and she was sure of the man's height and weight. We believe it was Martin."

"I think I would like to speak with her at some point. Did she note down the numberplate of the motorbike of the courier who dropped it off?"

Callum shook his head. "I'm afraid not, and there was no reason she would. It was a normal drop-off, like so many others she had overseen. Helen wasn't to know that the package would end up killing two people. It sounds like she manages that little post office on her own most of the time. She deals with shop and post office customers alike. That makes it less likely she would remember someone unless they stood out to her."

"I know... I was clutching at straws."

"Something else we found out..." Dai swivelled his chair round to face them. "Simon Mason, the base player with Rothwell's band, The Stoney Bastions, goes by the name of Simes. He has a history of going on anti-capitalist marches and is well known in activist circles under his nickname."

"Really?" Yvonne perched on the edge of Callum's desk. "Any criminal activity?"

Dai nodded. "He has eight previous offences of criminal damage, three of which were committed on marches. The others were for trashing hotel rooms, for which other band members were also convicted back in the eighties and nineties."

"When did he commit the offences on the marches?"

"Two were in two-thousand-and-eight, at the height of the banking crash, and the other was in two-thousand-seventeen. There are rumours he was involved in more, but wasn't caught for anything."

"So, relatively recent..." The DI pursed her lips. "Has he written anything down about these marches? Or said anything on record concerning his beliefs about capitalism?"

"He has spoken out against the wealth gap and suggested boycotting companies with unethical practices. He appears to have a real bee in his bonnet over income disparity. "

"What about violence? What is his position on that? Just property? Or people too?"

"There was nothing in the articles discussing violent

action, but some of the bands' songs include lyrics about the poor working man and rioting."

"Really?"

"Going through all this stuff is why I was in so early this morning." Dai grimaced. "I persuaded Callum to help me out. Their song-writing has been prolific. It's taking forever to go through it all."

"Well, I am impressed. Keep up the good work. Can you do me a favour when you have a chance? Can you set up an interview with Helen Turpin, the girl from Tynderwen post office?"

"Will do."

"That's great. Thank you. I am going to pay another visit to Riverdale, as I understand Rothwell and his band are at the mansion until next week. I want to question them about the anti-capitalist marches they have taken part in and their lyrics. Dewi can come with me."

"Right you are, ma'am."

"If you can prepare a summary of what you have found so far, I'll take it with me."

"No problem..."

As Yvonne was about to leave the station with Dewi, a call came through from Geoff Taylor of the NCA.

Callum handed her the phone.

"Yvonne Giles..."

"Hi, it's Geoff." There was something soothing about the gravelly voice on the other end. "I'm calling about the attempted bombing at Welshpool court last week."

"I thought you might contact us." She pressed the phone hard to her ear.

He continued. "I know Counter Terrorism intend looking at the device, but I wanted your thoughts on this perpetrator. As I understand it, you have him on CCTV?"

"We have someone on CCTV, yes. I can't say at this stage whether it is the actual perpetrator. For all we know, the guy in our footage could simply be another courier or cog in the wheel. However, I can tell you the device would not have gone off, anyway. Our perpetrator, whoever he is, didn't secure the live wire well enough. We think it came loose when the court administrator threw the package into the street. I thought you would have looked at the bomb footage by now? The army filmed its contents."

"We haven't had a chance yet. Is the device with forensics?"

"As far as I know, unless Counter Terrorism has taken custody of it already. Listen, you should probably speak with Sergeant Denholm of the Army Logistics Corps. He was the bomb disposal expert who was to disarm the device that day, and told me the live wire had broken free of the mechanism, rendering it a dud. He knows as much about the bomb as anyone, I would say."

"That's useful, thank you."

"We think the same motorcycle guy took the Riverdale package to the postoffice from where Martin Dawes picked it up. The black outfit was identical. Like I say, we don't know that he is the perpetrator, but we are working hard to find him."

"Great, well, I will let you go. I am hunting down the Welshpool device so we can compare it to the remnants we got from the first one. I'll speak to you later." His phone clicked off.

Dewi caught up with her as she handed the phone back to Callum. "Are we ready?" He asked.

"Yes, let's go. I want to speak with Simes on his own, if I can."

"You want me to keep the others occupied?" He asked, putting on his tweed jacket.

"Please."

7

A STON(E)Y RECEPTION

The DI and Dewi had been waiting in their stationary car for seven minutes in searing heat, before Peter Davies waved them through the newly repaired gates. He announced the detectives to the residents over the intercom.

Having parked their vehicle in front of the steps up to the house, they waited again for the door to be opened.

Dewi checked his watch. "What on earth are they doing in there?" he asked, moving further into the shade of the porch.

"Maybe they are busy hiding evidence?" she answered, only half in jest.

As they waited, Yvonne felt a sense of unease creeping up her spine. Something was off. Something she couldn't quite put her finger on. Perhaps it was the way the house seemed to loom over them, casting a shadow that grew darker with every second. Or maybe it was the way the air felt heavy and suffocating, as if the oxygen had been sucked out of it. Perhaps it was because they had arrived during the hottest part of the day. And the DI could see in her mind's eye the wrecked van with the bodies of two men who had gone to work on that fateful morning and never returned. Two families deprived of their loved ones. She pressed her lips together before muttering, "Open the damn door."

Dewi was about to suggest they leave when the entrance finally opened.

Rothwell stood unapologetic in the doorway. Sleeves rolled up; chin covered in stubble, and heavy bags under the eyes, he looked like he had been up half the night. He glanced from one to the other of them. "Yes?"

The DI raised a brow. "May we come in? I did phone ahead to say we'd be paying you a visit."

He tutted. "Jeanette said someone had rung."

This didn't bode well. Yvonne stepped forward, hand on her hip. "Is everything okay, Mr Rothwell? You seem tense."

The singer frowned. "I had a late night, that's all. I suppose you had better come in."

As they entered, Yvonne still couldn't shake the feeling that something wasn't right. The air inside was thick with the scent of cigarette smoke and alcohol. She looked around, her eyes scanning for other members of his entourage.

"Can I get you anything to drink?" Rothwell asked.

Dewi declined, but Yvonne accepted a glass of water, aware this would give them a few moments' grace. As Rothwell left to fetch the drink, Yvonne crossed over to a piece of paper on the coffee table. She leaned in to get a better look.

It was a receipt for a storage unit. The name on the receipt was not Rothwell's. She snapped a quick photograph with her mobile.

"Is there something you wanted to look at?" the singer asked, startling her. He had returned with Yvonne's water and was standing in the doorway.

"I would like a chat with you, if I may?" Dewi interjected, giving the DI a wink as Rothwell handed her the glass. It was his way of telling Yvonne he would keep everyone occupied so she could talk to Simon Mason on his own.

"Is Simes around?" She asked while Rothwell led them to the sitting room.

"He is... I think he went to the kitchen to fix himself a sandwich."

"Do you mind if I look for him?"

He shrugged. "Help yourself. Keep going down the corridor, and it is the second-to-last door on your left."

She gave a nod to her DS and set off down as directed.

Passing room after room, the DI couldn't help but feel she was intruding on something private. The dimly lit hallway added to the eerie atmosphere in the house. Yvonne's grip on her water glass tightened as she approached the second-to-last door. She told herself she felt as she did only because two men had lost their lives in the grounds outside. She took a deep breath and knocked on the kitchen door.

"Yes?" Simes' voice sounded hoarse. He must have indulged in the night's heavy drinking with Rothwell.

"It's DI Yvonne Giles. I was hoping to have a chat with you."

He appeared in the doorway, grey hair mussed; jeans and tee shirt crumpled like he had slept in them, and reeking of cigarettes. "Do you have to?"

"It shouldn't take too long."

He sighed, looking at her with bloodshot eyes. "Fine."

"Late night was it?" she asked, as he led her to bar stools at the hardwood kitchen counter. The surface sported several unwashed glasses and plates of half-eaten finger-food.

"You could say that."

She pulled out a stool and sat, waiting for him to do the same. Through the large windows opposite, she has a view of the picturesque landscaped gardens at the rear of the house.

He perched on the stool next to hers, leaning on the counter and rubbing his eyes.

"I'm curious about your band's history," she began. "You've had quite a chequered past."

He lifted his gaze to her, narrowing his eyes. "What do you mean?"

"I understand you've been in trouble in the past for causing damage to buildings and property?"

"Oh, that..." He sighed. "Yeah, well, I'm in a band, aren't I? It's kind of expected."

"Expected by whom?"

"By our fans... try to name me a rock guitarist who hasn't been in trouble for something?"

"So, you are the lead guitarist?"

"I play bass guitar." He frowned, as though she should know that already.

"Did you get in trouble only because you thought you should for the fans?"

He shrugged. "It was mostly when I was younger. Drink, substances... You know, it was the way we released all that nervous energy. The record companies didn't mind too much. You know what they say... Any publicity is good publicity. We've been on the front pages more times than we've had hot dinners."

"You seem proud of that fact."

"I never caused damage in a place where I couldn't afford to fix it." He swivelled from side-to-side on his chair, like a teenager might when given a dressing down by a parent.

"Causing damage to hotel rooms creates not only a financial burden for the owners, but stress for the people having to deal with it. It is the lowest-paid staff who clear up the mess."

He didn't respond to that.

She rubbed her chin. "You feel for the poorest in society, as I understand it? You've been on marches with them protesting wealth disparity?"

"I've been on a few."

"And some of those were anti-capitalist marches?"

"Might have been, yes."

She glanced at her notes. "One of your offences involved throwing a brick through a plate-glass window?"

"What has that got to do with anything?"

"Another involved setting advertisement hoardings on fire in the street."

"I wasn't the only one doing that, and it was ten years ago."

"Your last offence was five years ago and, I admit, your reckless behaviour has become less frequent recently."

"Yeah, well, the old joints don't work as well as they used to." He grinned. "It's hard to be an anarchist when you can't run."

"Are you unhappy with society?"

"I'm upset at how things are run sometimes; the unfairness of things, yes. Billionaires living in big houses, while the poor in society, struggle to pay their rent."

"Big houses like this one?" She scoured his face.

He scowled. "Very funny."

"Well, you're not exactly practising what you preach."

"It's the principle of it. We are a band, not a big corporation."

"Oh yes, that makes it all right then." The DI grinned to soften the jibe. She needed his cooperation.

"Do you mind if I smoke?" he asked. "I can vape if you prefer?"

"I would rather you vaped, if possible?" She nodded.

"I'll be right back."

She watched him leave the room before checking her watch and turning her gaze back towards the large sash windows. The view swept over the landscaped world beyond, and the DI wondered what had led to the band drinking for most of the night. Was it an unavoidable consequence of the tragic events of two weeks before?

"I'm back." Simes strode into the room, retaking his seat at the counter. "I can see you have me down as some sort of anarchist, but I only ever got involved in things in the heat of the moment. If I had stopped to think, I probably wouldn't have done any of it." He vaped, blowing the steam above his head.

"I understand the band's song lyrics are written mostly by yourself and Rothwell. Is that right?"

"Yeah, we have written most of our songs ourselves."

"Who writes more, you? Or Rothwell?"

"Dean writes the soppier songs." He pulled a face. "I create the bolshy stuff."

"What about the lyrics calling for the breaking down of society and rebuilding it better? Who wrote those?"

"Er... That was mostly me."

"Do you feel the things you write?"

"Sometimes... Mostly... Yeah, I suppose I do."

"Would you take society apart and rebuild it if you could?"

He shrugged. "Maybe..."

"What about the lyrics concerning the so-called 'crimes of the West'? Did you write those?"

"Yeah."

"The ones asking for a utopia to replace the West?"

He reddened. "I wrote those lyrics, yes."

"What would you replace it with? I'm curious... Our ancestors worked hard to build what we have. We have arguably never had it better. This isn't ground zero. If society failed, we would likely struggle to eat, clothe, and house ourselves. Wouldn't you agree?"

He frowned. "What do you want me to say? Where is this going?"

"I'm simply trying to gauge the strength of your feelings on these matters, given the lyrics of your songs."

"Do you think I blew up the front gates as some sort of protest?" He raised a brow, his expression imperious. "Really? Do you think I would be that stupid? I quite like my life, thank you. I don't fancy living the rest of it behind bars."

"I'm not accusing you of anything, Mr Mason. I want to know your views, and how strongly you believe those things."

"Not enough to blow up two people." He scowled. "If you think it was me, you are barking up the wrong street. Even if I really held those beliefs, it doesn't mean I would hurt people to achieve them. What do you take me for? I've never physically harmed anyone. I might have trashed the odd hotel room, and set a few hoardings on fire, but that doesn't make me a fanatic."

"I understand your band split for a while a few years back?"

He put down his vape cigarette and folded his arms. "Yeah, we did. What of it?"

"May I ask why?"

"Dean and I went through a patch where we just couldn't get on."

She cocked her head. "Why was that?"

"We couldn't agree on the direction we wanted to take the music. Things were getting stale, and I wanted to change our sound; modernise it, you know?"

"What happened?"

"We had a bust up during one of our practices. We were writing a new song, and couldn't agree on the way we wanted it to go. I ended up walking out and telling Dean to stuff it. I think my language was a little more choice than that, but you get the picture?"

"I do…"

"I regretted it pretty much straight away, but we didn't talk again for nearly three years. I had it in my head that I didn't need the others, and that I could go solo or join another band. But I couldn't, and the rest of The Stoney Bastions said they couldn't perform without me. So we got back together, did a comeback tour, and recorded our next album. It did pretty well, better than our stuff had done for a while. That was nearly five years ago. I think everyone needs a refresh sometimes. Ours did wonders for us."

"How do you guys get on now?"

He shrugged. "We have our moments, but I think we've all mellowed a bit in the last few years. There's more give-and-take now, I would say. Life is too short for strife."

"What were your thoughts when the van blew up outside?"

"I thought it was terrible that someone would put a bomb in a package like that. I mean, what if it had gone up in the house when we were all here? Don't get me wrong, I feel sorry for Ted's death, and that of the delivery guy, but it could have been so much worse. It could have taken the lot of us."

"Have you any idea who might have done this? Do you know anybody who has threatened this kind of action, even in an off-hand manner?"

He shook his head.

"Do you know anyone with the technical skills to do this sort of thing?"

"No."

"Can you think of anyone who the band has upset in the last few years?"

"Nope... Not really."

"Not really? What does that mean? You've upset someone, but not enough for them to want to hurt you?"

"Something like that, yeah."

"Who did you upset?"

"I can't remember but, I tell you what, I'll have a think about it and let you know." He looked at his watch. "I'm sorry. We are supposed to finish a song we are writing by tonight. We're in the studio tomorrow. I'd love to sit here chatting, but..."

"Very well." She climbed down from the stool. "I'll let you get on. But if you think of anyone who might have done this, or you hear anything you think we should know, I want you to contact us right away." She handed him her card. "You can leave a message if I don't answer. And if I don't answer, please leave one."

He accepted the card, placing it in his jeans' back pocket. "Sure... No problem."

As she walked down the corridor back to Dewi, Yvonne pondered what the bassist had said. He had the potential to commit drastic action, but she was not yet convinced he was their man. But something about this group didn't sit right with her. There was a lot more digging to do.

Yvonne pulled up in the yard outside of Drws Melyn Cottage in Meifod, seven miles north-west of Welshpool, in the valley of River Vyrnwy.

The cottage was a black and white two-story building, typical of those from the Tudor period. The front door was painted in bright yellow gloss. Dewi had informed her that Drws Melyn meant Yellow Door. She could see how the name made perfect sense.

Rhonda Edwards answered the doorbell, her greying hair tied back in a bun. She wore a flour-stained apron over a lilac cotton dress and sported a streak of flour on her cheek where she had pushed stray hair behind her ears.

"Mrs Edwards?" Yvonne cocked her head. "I'm DI Giles, Dyfed-Powys Police."

"Come in... I've been expecting you." Rhonda led the DI through the hall to her kitchen, where ceramic bowls of various sizes lay on a central pine table dusted with flour. "I'm baking today. I hope you don't mind?"

"Not at all." The DI removed her jacket as the heat from a small range made her swelter.

"I hope you don't get too hot." Rhonda pulled a wooden chair out for Yvonne to sit. "The window is open as wide as it will go to let out some of the heat. I get so hot baking in this weather. Ted loved fresh bread and buns." She sighed, her eyes filling up. "Now I make them for Keith when he gets home from school, and I save some for his sister for when she visits us."

"I'm so sorry for your loss..." The DI's gaze was soft. "How are the children?"

"They are bearing up... Keith is seventeen. He went back to school today after having two weeks off in mourning. He has his A-level finals next year. Sarah is twenty-one, and eight-and-a-half months pregnant. She's due to give birth in a couple of weeks. They cried for most of the first week after their father was killed. They were lost and in shock. We all were. I have helped them as best I can, and they have been offered counselling, which they have so far refused. Sarah is devastated that her child will never know his grandad. I have never seen Keith and Sarah hold each other so much. I'm baking to make things as normal as possible for my son when he gets home from school. But there is a hole in our lives which is impossible to fill. We are taking each day as it comes."

"Tell me about Ted... What was he like?"

"He was a really loving husband and father; our rock. He worked his socks off for us, and made sure we never went without. His job took a lot out of him. He often worked long shifts, but he would still have time for us when he got home, and would help the kids with their homework, or play with them while I cooked dinner. We were his world, and he was ours."

"How long had he worked for Dean Rothwell?"

Rhonda looked up at the ceiling as she thought about it. "It must be coming up to twenty years," she said, her gaze returning to the DI.

"That's a long time."

"It was."

"Did he enjoy working at Riverdale?"

"He did most of the time."

"Most of the time?"

"Well, sometimes things upset him. He wasn't usually one to complain at work, but he would get it off his chest when he came home by talking it through with me after the kids had gone to bed. He needed it so he could sleep."

"What sort of things made him unhappy?"

"There was stuff going on at work that he felt was unfair."

"Such as?"

"A colleague wasn't pulling his weight half the time. Ted sometimes worked extra shifts to cover for him, or had to work late because of him." Rhonda sighed. "It used to sap my husband's energy."

The DI tilted her head. "Are we talking about Pete Davies here?"

Mrs Edwards nodded. "Yes."

Yvonne remembered her conversation with the surviving guard. "I thought they were good friends?"

"Hah!" Rhonda blurted. "That is one way to look at it."

"But you have another?"

"Ted would get frustrated with Pete. I've even heard him swear when discussing him. And Ted wasn't one for cursing, but it was getting to him. And there were other little things too, such as Pete leaving it to Ted to report problems when things went wrong."

"Such as?"

"Such as water leaks or repairs that were needed. Like all old buildings, Riverdale has its issues, and Rothwell is away a lot. These problems mount up. Ted suggested they employ a building maintenance manager, but Rothwell wasn't keen. So it was left to him and Pete to report any problems that occurred. Rothwell would almost never arrange for them to be sorted. He would instead ask his security staff to make the phone calls. It so often ended up with Ted ringing round workmen and utility companies, because Peter told him he was no good at it."

"Was Davies aware of how upset he was making your husband? Did Ted have a conversation about it with him?"

Rhonda nodded. "Only a few weeks ago, Ted warned Pete that he would go to Rothwell and tell him what had been going on. Pete begged him not to say anything and promised he would do better."

"And did he?"

"For about a week, and then he went back to his old habits."

"I see..."

"There was a burglary at the property a while back. Jewellery and paintings were taken. Ted was extra vigilant after that, but he would tell me how Pete had far too casual an attitude towards security. My husband felt Pete did as little as he could get away with."

"Who occupies the gardener's cottage?"

"No-one lives there anymore. Rothwell sometimes rents it out or lets his friends stay there for a break, but often it is used purely as a temporary storage for equipment."

"Did Ted ever carry out his threat to tell Rothwell about Pete?"

Rhonda shook her head. "No, and he was the sort of man that would find it very difficult to tell on a colleague, even one as lazy as Pete Davies could be."

"Do you think it would have made a difference if he had?"

"Perhaps..." Mrs Edwards rubbed her forehead. "But with Dean Rothwell and his estate management, who knows? He is away so often, you see. I suspect Ted would have dealt with the same problems five years from now. I don't think Pete has it in him to change."

"It sounds like your husband was a patient man, but that patience was running thin."

"It was, but I think Ted would have continued to forgive and forget until it killed him."

The oven timer beeped, causing the DI to jump. She checked her watch, grabbing her jacket from the back of the chair. "I'm so sorry, Mrs Edwards. I have taken up enough of your time when you are busy. Thank you for your help."

"Do you think you will find whoever did this to my husband?" Rhonda turned off the timer before blowing her nose into a hanky.

"We are throwing everything we can at this." The DI nodded. "Officers from multiple disciplines are bringing their expertise to the case. I believe we can resolve it, and bring the perpetrator to justice."

"I saw there was another bomb left at the court. Looks like the person responsible won't stop until you catch him."

"That is why we are working tirelessly to stop them." The DI donned her coat. "Can I say once again how very sorry I am for your loss, Mrs Edwards? I will stop at nothing to catch whoever did this to your husband. You have my word."

As she left Rhonda to her baking, Yvonne brooded on Pete and the conversation she had with him regarding the closeness he had shared with Ted. Either Davies was delusional, or he had flat-out lied. Whichever the case, the DI was determined to understand what had gone on between the two security guards prior to Ted's death.

8

FAULTY DEVICES

W hen the DI arrived back in the office, she and Dewi grabbed a swift coffee to take back to their desks. Meanwhile, she informed him of what Ted's wife had said about Pete Davies.

"It sounds to me like Ted wasn't very well supported by the management." Dewi nodded.

"If there is any management at that house." Yvonne grimaced. "It sounds to me like Rothwell was leaving a lot for his security team to deal with. Ted was almost managing the place by himself, if what his wife told me was true."

"Well, I guess the band is on tour a lot. And, when they are at home, it seems to me Rothwell and friends spend a lot of time partying and recording songs. I suspect fixing and sorting stuff is somewhere near the bottom of their list."

"How did they all behave while I was talking to Simes?"

"It's hard to say." Dewi pulled a face. "Sometimes I felt they were exchanging knowing looks, and other times they appeared relaxed enough. Andy got up and paced the room a few times, but they were working on the songs for their new album. Apparently, they have a sound engineer who pops in when they are ready to record. His name is Kyle Waterman. He's thirty-two, and has been helping the band out for the best part of a decade. Started off working for them for free, apparently, as he wanted the experience."

Yvonne nodded. "Anyway, I want to speak to Davies again, and find out why he misled me regarding his friendship with Ted. They were not nearly as close as he would like us to believe."

"Yes, sounds like he is hiding something." The DS nodded.

The DI ran a hand through her hair, her eyes soulful. "Ted was about to become a grandfather, Dewi."

"His daughter is pregnant?" he asked, wide-eyed.

"She is due to give birth in two weeks. As if this situation wasn't awful enough... He was really looking forward to meeting the baby."

"Poor guy." Dewi sighed. "My God, what a mess."

Callum, pencil tucked behind his ear, interrupted their conversation. "Sorry to interject, but a suspicious package has been delivered to the manager of Morrisons supermarket in Newtown this morning. Bomb Disposal is on en route. Would you like myself and Dai to go down there?"

"Oh no, not another one..." The DI frowned. "No, it's okay, Callum. Dewi and I will go. I need you to look into the background of the surviving security guard at Riverdale, Peter Davies. I want to know if he has a record and, if so, what offences he has committed. Also, security staff often have a police or army background. I'd like you to look into whether he has anything like that in his history."

"Are you thinking he might have bomb-making skills?"

"I don't know, but he is now on my radar, so I'd like him checked out."

"No problem. We can start this afternoon." Callum took the pencil from behind his ear. "Go easy out there," he reminded them. "That van explosion was nasty. You don't want to get caught up in anything like that."

"Thanks." She grimaced. "We'll try not to."

WHEN THEY ARRIVED at Newtown Morrisons, off the Poole Road, they were met with a flood of traffic from the car park, as shoppers left the area in droves.

Uniformed officers had taped off the entrance next to Aldi, forcing leftover customers to abandon their vehicles and leave on foot.

Dewi parked in Aldi's car park, and they walked for the final fifty metres to the supermarket entrance.

The Army Logistics Corps had still not arrived, and the DI and Dewi had no choice but to wait until they had assessed the situation. They stood, faces tense, saying little as they waited.

The corps' signature van with its yellow stripe arrived from North Wales twenty minutes later. The occupants wasted no time getting to work donning protective gear; frowns of concentration on their faces.

Yvonne recognised Sergeant Denholm and gave him a wave.

He didn't wave back, appearing instead to look straight through her so deep was he in concentration. His unit disappeared into the supermarket, accompanied by their roving vehicle with its robotic arm.

The DI pressed her lips together, checking her watch. It was just after mid-day. She and Dewi stood next to some trollies under the shade of the overhang, biting their lips; hands in pockets.

After almost half an hour, the sergeant emerged, protective armour discarded, striding back towards his vehicle.

The DI chased after him. "Sorry to interrupt you..."

He paused, turning towards her.

"DI Giles, we met last week in Welshpool..."

"Ah yes..." He smiled for the first time. It brightened his face, and he looked ten years younger. "How are you?"

"I'm good, thank you. What are we looking at?"

He rubbed his chin. "It is a similar device to the one we saw in Welshpool. It was put together in the same way, and has the same issues."

She frowned. "What do you mean?"

"It has the makings of a proper device, but it wouldn't go off as it is."

"Live wire hanging loose?"

"Spot on. We confirmed it with our rover." He shook his head. "I think your bomber has become careless."

"I'm thinking that myself." She stepped back. "Thank you, Sergeant. I'll let you get on," she said, before heading back to Dewi.

"What have they found?" he asked, hands in pockets.

She relayed to him what Denholm had said, shaking her head. "I don't understand... Why go to all that effort, but get it all so wrong? It makes little sense. Something about this doesn't sit right, Dewi. Something is off."

"I'll admit, it is very odd," he agreed. "Maybe the bomber was in a rush, or he was disturbed by someone, and he rushed it."

"I guess that's possible, but it seems unlikely. Once, I could accept. But twice? Having been disturbed on a previous occasion, I would think he would be more cautious this time. And why send it if he isn't sure it will go off? We cannot blame the failure on someone throwing the parcel around this time. It makes me wonder if the bomber's aim was not to harm, but to frighten?"

Dewi nodded. "Maybe Counter Terrorism can shed some light? Or the NCA? We should check on their progress. I'd like to think they would keep us informed, but I've the feeling they won't give much away unless we ask."

She pursed her lips. "I'll make a few calls when we get back."

PETE DAVIES ATTENDED the station seven minutes late for his interview with Yvonne and Dewi.

Given what she had been told by Ted's wife, Rhonda, the DI was not surprised. She made a point of looking at her watch, letting him know his tardiness has not escaped her.

"Good afternoon, Peter," she said, as she lead him into the interview room; observing the beads of sweat on his temple and the tremor in the arm which held his coat. "Please, take a seat. We're just waiting for my colleague, DS Hughes, to join us."

"Fine." He grunted as though to clear his throat, but Yvonne suspected it was more about covering nervousness. She set about organising her papers, not looking up, allowing him time to settle and drink a little water.

Dewi rushed in, giving the DI a nod before settling down next to her.

"Welcome, Mr Davies." Yvonne sat back in her chair. "Thank you for coming in at such short notice. I know you have to get back to work, so we will keep this as brief as we can."

"Thank you." He licked his upper lip, eyes flicking from the DI to Dewi and back.

"Pete... Can I call you that?"

"Yes, of course you can." He rubbed his forehead with the back of his hand.

"Tell me about your working relationship with Ted. How did you two get on? What did your typical work day entail?"

"We got on great. We really did. Yeah, we did..." He nodded for emphasis, but his chest heaved, and his sighs belied his affirmations.

"And how would you begin your day at Riverdale?"

"Well, it would depend if our employer was home... If he was, we would usually arrive around eight in the morning to do the first checks of the day. We would split up, with one of us checking the grounds and vehicles, and the other checking the house and smaller buildings. We would meet up for tea break, and then one of us would be in charge of the gates and grounds, and the other would monitor the house."

"What about when your employer wasn't home?"

"We would take it in turns to do a night shift. We did those solo. Whoever worked the night shift would usually go home after the morning tea break. So we would start the day shift together to discuss any important issues during the handover."

"I'm trying to understand the hours you each worked here." The DI frowned in concentration. "So, say you worked the night shift..."

"Okay..."

"You would stay until when? Mid-morning?"

"Yes, I would stay until the morning checks had been done. Then Ted would take over from me while I went home to catch up on sleep, and so on. I would come back at eight the next evening for the night shift again. And Ted would go home."

"So you would both be working long shifts while your employer was away. Am I right?"

"Yes, that's correct. We were paid time and a half for a night shift."

"What happened when Mr Rothwell was home?"

"In that case, we both worked during the day, usually eight in the morning until six at night. When Mr Rothwell was home, there would be a lot more comings and goings. Sometimes we worked late if Mr Rothwell wanted help with something specific, and time ran on. We didn't get paid any extra for extending a day shift."

"Were you happy with those hours? Was Ted?"

"We were happy with the money we were getting. I am getting even better money at the moment until we have found a replacement for him."

"Do you get tired?"

"It can be exhausting, yes. Some weeks more than others, especially when Roth-, Mr Rothwell is away. There is always some problem or other."

"Did Ted get tired?"

Davies shrugged. "I guess so."

"Did he talk to you about being feeling fatigued?"

"He might have mentioned it in passing."

"Did he ever talk to you about how the work was divided up? Did he complain about how much he was doing compared to yourself?"

Davies's eyes narrowed. "What are you getting at here?"

"People close to Ted tell me he felt he was covering for you a lot. Would you agree with that? Or do you feel it is unfair?"

"I pulled my weight." He leaned back in the chair, brushing off his thighs as though they were covered in dust.

"What about the issues you talked about? If problems arose, such as water leaks, who did most of the ringing round to get them dealt with?"

Davies scowled. "Ted was better than me on the phone. He knew how to organise other people. I let him do it because I thought he was good at it."

"How did Ted feel about that? Did you ask him? Did he tell you?"

"You make it sound like he was hard done by."

"Was he?"

"I don't think so, no."

"What did he think?"

He shrugged.

"You see... I think he discussed it with you and asked you to pull your weight."

Davies shook his head.

"Further, I believe he warned you of his intention to report you to Mr Rothwell if you didn't buck your ideas up."

"He wouldn't have done that... He wouldn't have followed through with it."

"Is that why you took advantage?"

"I didn't mean to take advantage." Davies rubbed his forehead. "Okay, sometimes I was late. Life gets in the way, you know? He might have grumbled about it, but it would be forgotten soon enough. And I would have done the same for him. I would have covered for Ted."

"Except you never had to..."

"But I would have done if needed."

"I understand Ted threatened to report you again the week before he died? It seems he had reached the end of his tether?"

"He was always at the end of his tether. It doesn't mean he would have actually gone to Rothwell. I didn't believe he would, anyway. Ted wasn't like that."

"Did you feel any guilt, Mr Davies?"

"For what, exactly?"

"For Ted being at the end of his rope?"

"I would feel guilty if I was late, but we got on with things and it soon passed. Anyway, we had other things to talk about in the weeks before the explosion."

"Like what?"

"Like how Rothwell would react when he found out his missus was having it away with his best friend." Davies sat back in his chair, a smug look on his face. "We thought there would be fireworks, but we didn't expect an explosion."

Yvonne scratched her head, taking on board this new information. "Are you telling me Jeanette has been having a relationship with Jason Leyland behind Rothwell's back?"

Davies folded his arms. "Yeah, that is pretty much it. Jeanie and Jace were an item. They have a thing going on."

"When did you find out? How did you find out? How do you know they are having an affair?"

"Ted saw them in a clinch one time when he went into the house, when Rothwell was out. They separated right away, but they knew he had seen them. Ted felt there was an awkwardness after that, especially between him and Jace. I was all for telling Rothwell what was going on. I don't believe in women cheating behind their men's backs. But Ted made me swear not to say anything. He didn't want any trouble. He didn't think it was our place to report them."

"And did you speak to Rothwell about it?"

"No."

"What did Ted tell you about the awkwardness between him and Jason? What form did it take? In what way was their relationship difficult?"

"Jace's attitude towards Ted changed completely. Even I could see that. Leyland watched Ted like a hawk whenever he went anywhere near him."

"Did Jason discuss any of it with Ted? Did he ask him not to say anything about what he had seen?"

"I don't know, but there was a menace about Leyland after that, even with me. It was like he wanted us to know he'd break our necks if we breathed a word."

"But he didn't actually say that to you?"

"He didn't need to. It was obvious from his body language: clenched fists, and red face."

"I see. Do you believe Jason Leyland might have hurt Ted?"

"If you're asking me if he would have blown him up, I wouldn't know. Probably not, but people are capable of all sorts of things you wouldn't expect." He grinned. "There's nowt as queer as folk, as they say."

The DI checked her watch. "You need to be back at work in half an hour," she reminded him. "I suggest you leave now so you can be there on time."

"Right." He grabbed his jacket from the back of his chair. "Just let me know if you need any more information about the goings on at Riverdale. You'd be surprised what us security guards see." He tapped the side of his nose while winking at her.

She stifled a shudder. "We will contact you if we need anything further, Mr Davies."

"What do you make of that?" Dewi asked, after showing Pete out of the building.

"I wouldn't trust that man further than I could throw him. But do I think he is the Riverdale bomber? Probably not, but he is on my radar, Dewi. He is most definitely on my radar."

9

THE MAN IN BLACK

That afternoon, the team got together to discuss the latest developments in the case.

Yvonne held up a photograph of the receipt she had seen at Riverdale for a storage unit in the name of a Terrence White. "This may be something or nothing, but this receipt was left on a table in the library at Riverdale. It is for two months' rent of a storage unit housing unspecified items. The name could be fake, as we could not find a Terrence White connected to either Rothwell or Riverdale. I do not wish to ask Rothwell about it yet, as I don't want to alert him to the fact we are looking into the unit. I wouldn't want him getting rid of anything before we have a chance to investigate."

"It wouldn't surprise me to hear that Rothwell was using a false name." Callum shrugged. "He's worth a bob or two, and his name on the books could attract break-ins from criminals, fans, or even the paparazzi. He's probably taking extra precautions, as many celebrities would."

The DI nodded. "Absolutely, but if this is Rothwell's storage, I would be interested to know what is in there. Dai, could you look into it for me? Have a chat with the company, Baron's Storage, and see what you can glean from them regarding how long Rothwell has had the unit, if you can? Before I discuss this with him, I would like as much background information as possible."

"Sure, no problem," Dai agreed. "What are you thinking? Do you suspect him of keeping bomb-making equipment there?"

Callum sniggered.

Yvonne shot the DC a stern look. "You might laugh, but what if he has?"

"There have been two other devices found since the explosion at Riverdale. We think the bomber is choosing places at random to either push forward an anarchist agenda, or make it look like he is..."

"Why would someone want to only look like they have an agenda?" Callum pushed his hands deep into his pockets.

"I can see why you may doubt it is the singer." The DI sat on the edge of the table behind her. "But here's the thing... Only one of those devices went off. That was the bomb sent to Riverdale. The other two did not. And, what is more, they never would have. Whoever put the other two bombs together was careless... Too careless. He didn't bother checking the live wire connections. What self-respecting bomber does that? I am not buying that he made the same mistake twice. You know what I am thinking? The second and third devices were never meant to go off. I have a feeling they were sent to the court and a supermarket to throw us off the scent. I am going to run this idea past Taylor and Hanlon from the NCA, and see what they say. What do you guys think?"

Dewi pursed his lips. "You could be right, but that would mean the bomber is someone close to Rothwell."

"Right, and maybe the singer has been targeted by the perpetrator before? We know there was a burglary at the house a few years back, and the perpetrators were never caught. Perhaps Rothwell is keeping valuables in storage in case it happens again, especially in view of the explosion. But, regardless of whether he is the bomber, I would still like to know more about the unit and what he is keeping there. He has a huge and ancient house. I would have thought there would be plenty of nooks and crannies to hide his valuables if he wanted them at home."

Callum cocked his head. "What if Rothwell isn't the one using the storage? Any of them could have given a false name to Baron's. It's easy for someone in their position to get a false ID good enough to fool someone on the front desk of a local company, especially if they paid cash up front. No bank account for anyone to cross check. And I shouldn't imagine any of Rothwell's crowd are short of a few quid."

The DI nodded. "Perhaps we should discuss it with the singer. I can simply say I spotted the receipt there the other day and was curious. Whether he knows about it should be fairly obvious from his reaction. But before we do any of that, we need to know what's in that storage, in case he shifts it."

"We're investigating a double murder, and the occupants of Riverdale are on our suspect list. I say we pop along to Baron's and ask them what is being held there. If we run our suspicions past Llewelyn, he may agree to us getting a warrant for a search."

"But then we alert Rothwell and friends."

"Yes, but if we have a warrant, we can keep them from

removing anything before we have examined whatever is in there."

The DI nodded. "We'll discuss it with the DCI... Dai, can you get on to bomb disposal and forensics? I doubt very much the perp will have left fingerprints or DNA on any of the devices, but we need the results of any tests ASAP. Just be sensitive to anything else going on. We don't want to interfere with anything Counter Terror is up to. I'll speak to the NCA, we should be all right there. I think they were about ready to hand the case over to us, anyway. Can I leave it with you?"

"You certainly can." Dai gathered his notes together. "I'll let you know what we've found later."

YVONNE AND DEWI arrived at the Tynderwyn Village Post office a little after eleven in the morning. The shop was empty, save for Helen Turpin, the twenty-two-year-old shop assistant. She was the one who had witnessed the mysterious motorcyclist in a black helmet leave the parcel addressed to Weshpool Court.

Yvonne held up her badge. "Good Morning, Ms Turpin... DI Giles, Dyfed-Powys Police. We're here to talk to you about the man in the black motorcycle helmet who left a parcel with you last-"

"Oh, yes." The dark-haired, slender young woman walked out from behind the counter. "I've been waiting for you."

"Can you tell us what happened, and describe the man for us?" Yvonne leaned forward, her eyes focused on the girl. Dewi pulled out his notepad.

Helen took a deep breath, her expression filled with a

mix of anxiety and relief, as though she had been waiting to get it all off her chest. "It was last Thursday, around noon. I was tending to another customer when this man walked in wearing a black helmet that covered his face. It seemed odd to me, and I guess it made me a little uncomfortable. I realised he must be a courier, and I assumed he was in a hurry and that was why he had not removed his helmet. It was particularly his visor, which made me uneasy. It was dark and pulled down. I couldn't see his eyes. I could see the parcel was heavy, and asked if he could leave it next to the counter for the delivery company to pick up. I informed him he could. He told me the fee was pre-paid, and I could see there was a printed label on it. He didn't thank me. In fact, now I think of it, he said very few words at all... Like he didn't want to. Like he had a job to do and didn't want to get involved in conversation or the like. I remember I suggested I help the driver who picked it up to carry it to his van, as he looked like he was straining with it."

"Did you help?"

"No, he managed it himself, like the biker did, but I could see it was heavy."

Yvonne nodded.

Dewi scribbled down the information in his book.

"And what did the man who dropped off the parcel look like? Can you provide a description?"

Helen furrowed her brow, recalling the details. "He was average height, around five-feet-ten, or so. It was hard to gauge his age because of the helmet, but I would guess he was in his thirties or forties. I have to say that guess could be wrong. I couldn't see the skin on his hands. That's how I usually judge age, but he was wearing a biker's leather gloves. He had an average build, and I remember his voice being deep and muffled through the helmet. Unfortunately,

I couldn't see any distinguishing features since his face was completely covered."

Yvonne contemplated this, forming a mental image of the man in black. "Did he exhibit any unusual behaviour or say anything that stood out? Did you note anything behind his dark visor?"

Helen hesitated for a moment, her eyes darting to the side as she retraced the encounter in her mind. "Well, now that you mention it, he seemed tense, almost agitated. He said little, apart from asking to leave the parcel with me. But as soon as he put it down on the floor, he bolted from the shop. It was as if he couldn't wait to get away."

Dewi chimed in, his voice calm and composed. "Did you notice anything particular about the parcel? Anything at all?"

Helen shook her head, her eyes widening. "Only that the courier strained as he placed it on the floor. I wasn't surprised by that, as I could see it was from a furniture company. I suspected there was a lot of bubble-wrap inside the outer packaging. There were no markings other than the label, which had been laser printed in black ink. I would guess the weight was about the same as a sack of potatoes."

Yvonne rubbed her chin, pursing her lips, deep in thought.

Dewi closed his notebook. "Thank you, Ms Turpin. You've been very helpful. If you think of anything else or if you remember any additional details, please contact us."

Helen nodded, a mix of curiosity and concern flickering in her eyes. "Of course. I'll let you know if anything else comes to mind."

As Yvonne and Dewi made their way back to their car, Yvonne couldn't shake the nagging feeling there had been more to this encounter. The mystery of the parcel and the enigmatic man in the black helmet had deepened, leaving them with more questions than answers. On one hand, the man had wanted his identity hidden. On the other, his demeanour and manner of dress had garnered attention from the shop assistant because it was unusual. Had he actually wanted to stand out?

10

A RISKY AFFAIR

J ason Leyland waited in the reception area of Newtown police station, wearing a Stoney Bastions cap on backwards over his sparse grey hair. His neatly trimmed goatee was darker than the locks sticking out from under his cap. When he took it off, there appeared to be more strands in the frayed edges of his sleeveless denim jacket than there were hairs on the top of his head.

Yvonne collected Rothwell's friend, leading him to interview room two, where Dewi was busy readying their paperwork. "Please, take a seat," she directed the musician, pulling a chair out from under the table. "We have asked you here to discuss the explosion at the Riverdale mansion, and to ask you what you know of it?"

He grunted, clearing his throat, his eyes darting from one detective to the other. "I only know what I heard while we were on tour. It was a shock to everyone. I couldn't believe it... When we got back, and I saw the damage myself, I was horrified. None of us could believe that two people had died when the bomb went off. I think I actually went into shock. I didn't know what to do with myself. My legs literally turned to jelly. Who could have done it? Who could have tried to hurt us? I reckoned the bomb was supposed to go off inside the house, and not in the van parked outside. I believed Ted was an accidental victim."

Yvonne leaned forward, her gaze fixed on Jason's eyes. "Mr Leyland, we understand the shock and horror you must have felt when this happened. Our focus is on finding the person responsible. We are looking at this from every angle, so anything you remember from that time could be important. Have you spoken to Jeanette about it all?"

Leyland's eyes widened; a flicker of surprise danced across his face. "Jeanette? No, why would I? I mean, we all discussed it as a group. That's only natural. But I haven't spoken with Jeanie about it on her own. When we are on tour, we don't really speak much. I'm too busy with gear and technical stuff." He narrowed his eyes. "Why are you asking about Jeanie?"

Yvonne maintained a steady gaze. "We believe there is a connection between you and Jeanette. Witnesses have reported seeing the two of you together on more than one occasion."

Leyland's face paled, and he shifted uncomfortably in his seat. "I... uh... Well, we... We are just friends. I mean, we know each other, but there is nothing romantic between us."

Yvonne raised an eyebrow, her voice calm but firm. "Are you sure about that, Mr Leyland? We have eyewitnesses who have seen you in each other's arms, and their account suggests a more intimate relationship."

His face creased. He exhaled loudly, his teeth bared. "Alright, alright... We had a fling. It wasn't serious, just an affair. But it ended months ago. I didn't want trouble for Jeanette or Ted."

Yvonne nodded, noting his mention of the dead security guard. Something she had not done on purpose. Leyland had confirmed his awareness that Ted had seen him and Jeanie together. "Thank you for your honesty, Jason. It's essential for us to establish the facts and events leading up to the explosion. How does Jeanie feel about it all? Do you know?"

Leyland's gaze dropped to the floor, a mix of guilt and regret washing over his face. "I didn't want any of this. Neither of us did. Jeanie and I got caught up in something we couldn't control. But I wouldn't wish harm on anyone. You believe me, don't you?" He scoured Yvonne's face, his eyes round. "You don't think I arranged the bomb to get rid of Dean, do you? I care about Jeanie, but not enough to kill my best friend."

"What about the man who had witnessed you together?"

"No. Absolutely not... You think I had Ted killed so he wouldn't report our affair to Dean? That is crazy. What kind of man do you think I am?"

She pursed her lips. "We only want the truth, Mr Leyland. We will find the person responsible for what happened, and bring them to justice, hopefully before anyone else gets hurt. Nothing in this case is straightforward, but that won't stop us from being relentless in pursuit of this perpetrator. So, if you know anything, it is best you tell us now."

He lowered his gaze. "I wish I did, but I don't."

"Does Dean know about your affair with his partner?"

Leyland shook his head. "He has said nothing to me. And I doubt Ted had the time to..." His voice trailed away.

"Had the time to what?" Yvonne raised a brow. "Tell Rothwell?"

He shifted uncomfortably in his chair. "Well, I just don't

think Ted would have had time to speak with him before we went on tour."

She leaned in. "I guess that's right... Ted was killed before he had the chance, eh?"

Leyland's face reddened.

"How do you know Ted didn't tell Dean over the phone?"

"I don't. I just don't believe he did because Rothwell would have gone ballistic at me if he had found out."

"Ballistic in what way?"

"I would have been out on my ear."

"Not out of the band, though? You are not a direct member of the band, are you?"

He scowled. "I would have been off the tour, and out of Dean and the Stoney Bastions' life."

"How would you have felt?"

"Devastated... Hopeless... Life wouldn't have been worth living. They are my life. That band has been all I have known since I left school. Dean and I have been best friends forever."

"How do you live, Mr Leyland?"

"Sorry?"

"How do you feed and clothe yourself? What is your job, exactly?"

He grimaced. "Er... I..."

"Yes?"

"I don't have a set job..."

"Then how do you get money?"

He ran a hand through his hair. "I do odd bits for Dean and the band, you know... I move gear and help stage hands put stuff together sometimes."

"Sometimes?"

"Often... I do stuff often."

"So Rothwell pays you a wage?"

"Maybe not a wage, as you would know it..."

"But he gives you money?"

"I have my bed and food, and he gives me cash, but it isn't a regular wage. It goes up and down, depending on circumstances."

"So you don't pay taxes?"

He ran a hand through his hair. "No."

"So you would have a lot to lose if Rothwell booted you from his circle?"

Leyland nodded, shifting his feet under the table.

"Did you send that bomb to Riverdale?"

"No." He shook his head, staring into the jug of water on the table.

"Did you arrange for someone else to send it?"

"No, of course I didn't."

"You wanted Ted out of the way?"

"Christ, no!"

"Or you wanted a distraction to take the security guard's mind off what he had witnessed?"

"What do you take me for?" Leyland put his head in his hands, elbows on the table. Tears dripped onto the tabletop. "It's all a mess. I never meant for any of this to happen. You can't help who you fall in love with. I haven't seen Jeanie romantically since we got back."

The DI nodded. "We will speak to Miss Dupont shortly."

"Can I go now?" He put his back cap on backwards before turning it around the right way. "I have told you everything I know. I'm sorry that isn't much."

"You can leave, but I'd like you to stay in the area."

"I'm not going anywhere."

"Good."

Leyland sighed, shoulders slumping. "I hope you find

what you're looking for. I would never have wanted to do this to Dean or anyone else. You must believe me. I am not responsible for Ted Edwards' death."

"Thank you for coming in." She nodded.

As Leyland left the room, the two detectives exchanged looks. Ted Edwards had frightened the life out of Jeanie and Jason, but was that the reason for the explosion at Riverdale? And, if it was, which one of them was responsible?

THE TEAM BRIEFING the following day was attended by both Geoff Taylor and Dave Hanlon from the NCA.

After Yvonne had run through initial business, she gave up the floor for them to apprise the room of findings regarding the origin of the bombs. The information relayed was more a confirmation of what the devices were not, rather than what they were or where they had originated.

"Our forensic team said they didn't resemble any of the devices from known criminal bomb-making factories." Geoff put up a slide, showing a basic schematic of the components and how they were arranged. "They were not made in the same way as any we've seen before. The principles are similar, but the parts, and the way they were put together, were not like those from gangs we have investigated in the past. Could it be a new operation? Sure, but we have no intelligence to suggest this is the case. We know our perp or perps are careful not to leave fingerprints or DNA of any sort while constructing these things... No sweat, hair, or skin flakes... Nothing. These people are wary of discovery. It suggests it isn't someone who is making explosives in a foreign country or coming into Britain for a time and leaving again. Those guys might not be so bothered about leaving traces. We believe this individual is connected to the area, likely living or working here, and would be identified by their DNA. That is why they are so careful. I'll hand you over to my colleague, Dave."

Hanlon stood up, moving to the front. "The word in the criminal fraternity is that these devices have garnered significant attention. The underworld is interested in their capabilities and construction." He paused for a moment, allowing his words to sink in.

The detectives in the room leaned forward, their expressions serious as they absorbed Dave's information.

He continued. "Our intelligence suggests a substantial sum of money changed hands to secure delivery of these devices. We don't know the perpetrators' motives yet, but it's clear they are taking immense risks and spending a lot of effort to secure these devices."

He projected a series of images onto the screen, showcasing known figures within criminal networks. "We identified several key players involved in this illicit trade. All deny involvement. Our teams are working hard to rule these characters in or out."

Yvonne interjected, her tone determined. "Two lives have been lost already. We can't allow another bomb to go off. Those responsible are likely known to Rothwell or his associates. We are still probing them. They know something, I am sure of it."

Hanlon nodded. "The problem is, we see nothing in their banking records to support that. All transactions have so far been accounted for. We're continuing to dig, but have found nothing so far."

Geoff Taylor stepped forward once again, his gaze focused and resolute. "We have a daunting job ahead, but we have the skills, experience, and expertise needed to find those responsible. Don't lose faith. We will do this, but it needs all of us focussed on the task. Keep on it."

The meeting concluded, and the other officers dispersed while Yvonne gathered her papers together.

Callum approached, his forehead frowning in concentration. "I thought you should know that Jeanette Dupont started a *Go-Fund-Me* for the fixing of their mansion gates."

"What?" Yvonne frowned. "The gates have been fixed already. And what about Ted and Martin's widows? Did they get a mention in the Go-Fund-Me? Will they benefit from this?"

He shook his head, his expression stern. "Not a whisper of them anywhere in the endless paragraphs whining on about the emotional impact of the blast on her and Rothwell. Ted is mentioned, but only in relation to their grief at losing a member of their staff."

"Unbelievable." The DI exhaled heavily. "The word narcissistic comes to mind... I'd like a word with Miss Dupont. We'll get her in for a chat."

11

FEMME FATALE?

Yvonne sat across from Jeanette 'Jeanie' Dupont, her piercing gaze locked onto the enigmatic woman sitting in front of her. The woman exuded an air of confidence, crossing her long legs as she leaned back in the chair. Flowing blonde hair cascaded over her shoulders, framing a flawless face that seemed untouched by the complexities of life.

Yvonne knew that beneath that poised exterior was a woman tangled in a web of secrets and intrigue. It was time to peel back the layers of deception and expose whatever else Jeanie might be hiding. Leaning forward, the DI fixed her gaze on the woman, her voice firm and direct. "Ms Dupont, do you know anything about the explosion that happened in the grounds of Riverdale?"

Jeanie raised an eyebrow, a smirk playing at the corners of her lips. "Wow, you have an active imagination, Inspector. I need a moment to take that in... Let me assure you, I don't know what happened that day, or why. I had nothing to do with any explosion."

Yvonne leaned back in her chair, studying the Dupont's

face. "We know you have been seeing Jason Leyland, behind the back of your partner, Dean Rothwell. Witnesses have observed you being intimate with your husband's best friend. Would you like to tell us your side of the story?"

A flicker of annoyance crossed Jeanie's eyes, quickly replaced by a renewed composure. "Detective, my personal relationships have nothing to do with the explosion. And they are nobody else's business. People's perceptions can be misleading, and rumours often distort the truth. You should know that as well as anyone."

The DI pressed on, her voice steady and deliberate. "But, Jeanette, your past reveals a pattern. You dated another rock star before Dean Rothwell, and it's not a secret that you had an affair behind his back, too. You have a history of being involved in tumultuous relationships. We are wondering if your complicated personal life provided the means and motive for what happened?"

Jeanie's expression hardened, her eyes narrowing in defiance. "You're grasping at straws, Inspector Giles. My personal life and past relationships have no bearing on any of this. I am well aware my independent wealth raises envy and suspicion in certain quarters. Jealousy is a pernicious thing, but it does not make me a criminal mastermind... For God's sake, give me some credit."

Yvonne leaned forward, her voice firm and authoritative. "Jeanette, we have evidence that a significant amount of money changed hands in relation to these bombs. You certainly possess the financial means to fund such an opera-tion. The question is whether you used your money to pay whoever carried out the attack?"

Jeanie's composure wavered; a glimmer of unease crossing the former model's features. Yvonne detected the subtle crack in the façade the woman had crafted. Whether

Jeanie was involved in the horror that took place at the mansion's front gates or not, the DI felt she was hiding something.

The DI delivered the final blow. "I understand you set up a *Go-Fund-Me* Jeanette. I must admit to being a little surprised, given that you already have money, that you would seek financial help to repair the gates. Do you not have insurance for the property?"

"We have insurance. I simply thought the extra could help us put everything back together."

"What about Ted's widow? Will she benefit?"

Jeanette scowled. "I know where you are going with this."

"You have a duty of care, surely? Given that you and Rothwell were Ted's employers?"

"How much we can donate to others very much depends on how much the fund generates. We haven't planned that far ahead."

"I'm sorry, but your efforts seem a little mercenary to me. Jeanette, I could understand you setting up a fund to help Rhonda Edwards, but to fix your gates? I am speechless."

Jeanie shrugged. "If people don't want to give, they won't, simple as that."

Yvonne pressed her lips together, rubbing her forehead. "Ms Dupont, whether it leads us to your doorstep or elsewhere, justice will prevail. I suggest you cooperate fully with our investigation going forward."

The woman leaned back, chin jutting out; one eyebrow raised. "Detective, I understand the need for this inquiry, but I assure you, you are barking up the wrong tree. I had no involvement in what happened, and I wouldn't want anyone harmed. Now, if you'll excuse me, I have somewhere I need to be," Jeanie continued, her voice cool and dismissive. "I have no more time to entertain baseless insinuations. If you have nothing concrete to connect me to what happened, I suggest you focus your efforts elsewhere. You are wasting your time with me."

Yvonne knew breaking through the model's tough exterior would require persistence and evidence. Rising from her chair, she fixed Jeanie with a steady gaze. "Jeanette, mark my words. We will find out who did this. The guilty cannot avoid justice forever." She walked out of the interview room, leaving Dupont alone with her thoughts; signalling for the constable on the door to show the woman out.

YVONNE AND DEWI sat across from Dean Rothwell in the interview room.

The ageing singer, a weariness in the lines etched on his face, toyed with the handle on the mug of tea he had requested.

The DI flipped through her papers before questioning him, a moment to observe his reactions under pressure.

She cleared her throat, her voice firm. "Mr Rothwell, can you tell us why you rent a storage unit under the name Terrence White? Explain why you would use a false identity for such a mundane transaction?"

Dean shifted uncomfortably in his seat, his eyes avoiding those of the detectives. "What storage unit?"

"It's a lockup at Baron's Storage on the outskirts of Welshpool."

"I don't know what you are talking about." He picked at his nails.

"So, if we go to Baron's and ask them about this unit, and

serve a warrant to go through the items inside, you will be in the clear, will you?"

"It's not what you think," he began. "Yes, I rent a unit under a pseudonym, but I need to for security reasons. I have valuables such as paintings, antiques, and other belongings that I want to keep safe. I don't want anyone to know there is anything in there worth stealing."

Yvonne and Dewi exchanged glances, their expressions a mix of skepticism and curiosity. The DI leaned forward. "Mr Rothwell, we can understand your desire to protect valuable possessions, but using a false identity raises questions. Can you explain why you felt someone would break into this secure location? Baron's have a policy prohibiting the release of names of customers to the public. You could have given your real name, surely?"

He jutted out his chin, forehead creased in a frown. "I have a hard time trusting people because of what happened in the past," he stated, sounding irritated. "My mansion was broken into a few years ago. Irreplaceable items were stolen. It left me feeling violated. I couldn't bear the thought of going through all that again. So, I rent a storage unit under a false name as an extra layer of security. It isn't illegal and, frankly, it is none of your damn business."

Dewi leaned forward, his tone empathetic. "We understand the desire for protection, Mr Rothwell. But using a false identity raises suspicion, especially given what happened at Riverdale. Someone blew up a van on your land. Perhaps you rented that unit in order to house bomb components?"

"That is ridiculous." He scowled at them.

"Would you have any objections to us looking inside the unit?"

"You have no right to invade my private spaces."

"We are requesting a search warrant."

Dean's face paled, his tone changing. "Look, I didn't mean any harm or deception by renting under a false name. Believe me... It was merely a way to get peace of mind. I can show you the unit myself, and the belongings I keep there. You'll see it's nothing illegal or dangerous."

"Great, we'll do that." Yvonne nodded.

"I will need a few days."

The DI leaned back, her eyes narrowing. "A few days to do what?"

"I left the keys at an apartment in London. I will need them sent to me."

"Do Baron's not have a spare key?"

He shook his head. "I requested they hand over all keys for the unit to me. I paid extra for that. They don't have a master key. It's how I ensure the safety of my possessions."

"We would like to see inside the unit."

"Fine." Rothwell sighed. "I'll arrange for the keys to be sent by tracked delivery."

"Thank you. We would appreciate that."

Rothwell ran his hands through his hair.

"How are things between yourself and Jeanie?" She asked, head cocked.

"They're fine." He frowned. "Why do you ask?"

Yvonne pressed her lips together, mulling over the right words, not wishing to cause unnecessary trouble between the couple. Still, she needed to know whether the singer had any inkling of his partner's affair with his best friend. "I apologise if my question seems intrusive, Mr Rothwell," she said, maintaining a calm and neutral tone. "We are searching for a motive behind the attack. If someone wished to harm you or your partner, you would want to know why, wouldn't you?"

Dean's guarded expression softened, though a flicker of concern showed in his eyes. "I understand your job, Detective. But why are you asking about Jeanie?"

Shee chose her next words carefully, treading a delicate path. "Jeanie has been a part of your life for some time. I can see you have powerful feelings for her. Does she feel the same way about you?"

His brow furrowed, his eyes glazing for a moment. "We have had our share of difficulties over the years, but right now, we're in a good place. We're working through some things, but overall, we are fine. I know she loves me, if that is what you are wondering?"

Yvonne nodded, rubbing her chin. "May I ask what things you have been working through?"

Dean pursed his lips, rubbing his chin. "Is there something specific you wish to know about my relationship with Jeanie? I feel you have something in your head already?"

Yvonne continued. "Is it about the explosion at Riverdale?"

"Not really."

"Have you been seeing someone else?"

"What?" He frowned. "Why would I be seeing someone else? I love her. God, she is the only one who keeps me sane. I don't know what I would do without her, and she would leave me if she had any inkling I was having an affair."

"But you said you were working through some things?"

He sighed. "There are problems with the house... It's an old building. I don't get on with things as fast as she would like. It's hard, you know, when you are away a lot and living out of hotel rooms. We have a housekeeper and security staff, but no maintenance man."

"Why don't you hire someone to fix things, instead of

relying on your security staff to spot and deal with any problems?"

"Because I would have to pay a full-time salary for someone who would only be needed occasionally. I mean, problems don't arise all the time, do they? But, when they do, the issues are often big ones in that house, taking a lot of time and effort to put right. Jeanie is a visual person. She likes the aesthetic to be just so. She cannot bear it when things go wrong. And I hate letting her down."

"Are there any other issues within the relationship? Anything else you are trying to iron out?"

"Such as?"

The DI shrugged. "You tell me?"

"No."

"You are sure about that?"

"What is this? Do you want for there to be problems with my relationship? Do you think my Jeanie had something to do with the attempted bombing of our home?" His face had reddened considerably. His hands were clenched on the table.

Yvonne sighed. "I wouldn't be doing my job if I didn't question things, Mr Rothwell. As you have said, someone tried to hurt you or damage your home. We believe the perpetrator may be hiding in your inner circle. It is therefore important for us to understand how you relate to significant others."

His mouth fell open. He sat there wide-eyed. "You think Jeanie had something to do with the explosion?"

The DI shook her head. "That is not what I am saying. We do not know who was responsible, but we have to get to the bottom of what happened before anyone else gets hurt. Everyone is a suspect until we rule them out."

He closed his mouth again. "I see."

"Have you received any threatening letters since the explosion? Anything giving an ultimatum or warning it will happen again if you don't comply? Any demands for money?"

He shook his head. "No."

"What about these close to you? Have they received anything?"

"Not that I am aware of, no."

"Would they tell you if they did?"

"I believe so."

"Very well then, Mr Rothwell, I think that will be all for the moment. Please let us have the keys to your lockup when convenient."

"Of course." He nodded, grabbing his jacket from the back of the chair.

Yvonne couldn't help feeling a pang of guilt. She had avoided revealing Jeanie's secret, but knew it would come out soon, anyway. Although not impressed with Jeannette as an individual, the DI felt it wasn't her place to expose the major flaw in their relationship. For now, her focus remained on the case and finding answers without causing further harm to their fragile dynamic.

"We should monitor that storage unit," she said to Dewi, as they made their way back to CID. "Rothwell could be lying about the whereabouts of his keys. If he has been up to no good, he may look to remove stuff before we have time to examine the place."

"Exactly my thoughts," he agreed. "I'll ask Dai to watch the place. If he talks to the management at Baron's, he should be able to access their CCTV."

"Good." She nodded. "If Rothwell is innocent, he will look at his friends more intently tonight. I think we may have put the wind up him, but we have to expose the cracks if we are to find out who is responsible for the bomb."

"I think you handled it well." Dewi nodded. "It won't hurt for him to pay more attention to what's going on in his life."

12

WHEAT FROM CHAFF

B aron's Storage was on an industrial site close to Welshpool train station and airport. The main office was a graphite-grey portable cabin with white steps up to the door. Through the windows, soft strains of music could be heard emanating from a radio.

Yvonne and Dewi climbed the stairs and knocked on the door.

It was opened by a dark-haired young woman in her mid twenties, in jeans and a red company tee shirt with the Baron's signature logo of a castle keep and keys. "Yes?" she asked, opening the door wider, her amber eyes curious and unsure.

The DI held up her badge. "Hello, I'm DI Giles and this is DS Dewi Hughes. We would like to ask you questions about a unit rented by a Mr Terrence White."

The woman opened her mouth to say something, but hesitated. She shifted her weight between her feet, glancing behind before returning her gaze to them. "I'm sorry. We're not supposed to discuss the units with anyone but key holders."

"We understand that." Yvonne nodded. "But we are police officers, and we have spoken with Mr White, explaining our need to see for ourselves what is stored inside."

"I see." The woman stepped back. "You'd better come in."

The room contained two large desks covered in stacks of paper, receipt copies, and general stationery equipment.

"Sorry, I don't know your name..." The DI walked towards the desk now occupied by the young woman.

"It's Delyth... Delyth Davies."

"Very well, Delyth, we understand that Mr White is storing household items in his unit. To prove we have his permission for this visit, we have a receipt here for his storage payment, signed by him, and his keys." She held them up. "As I understand it, these are the only keys to the unit."

The woman cast her eyes over the receipt before opening an A4 book, and swiping her finger down the pages as she flicked through the names. "Ah yes, I have it. You want number twenty-seven. I'll take you there."

"Thank you." Yvonne stepped back, allowing the woman to lead them down the steps and through the yard to the lockup.

She took them across a gravelled forecourt, and on to a tarmac area, where the units stood five abreast. They wandered down the side until they came to the row labelled twenty-five to thirty.

The girl pointed. "It's the middle one," she said before turning on her heel and leaving them to it.

"Thank you very much." The DI handed the key to Dewi. "Do you want to do the honours?"

"Sure." He turned the key in the lock, lifting the door on its rollers until it was high enough for them to walk in.

They squinted, their eyes adjusting to the dimly lit interior as they began a meticulous search of everything stacked on the concrete floor. Examining the high-end furniture, they scanned each piece for hidden compartments or signs of illicit activity.

As she examined a majestic antique armoire, Yvonne admired its intricate carvings. She ran her fingers along the smooth, aged mahogany. "This is a remarkable piece..." Her gaze lingered on the ornate patterns. "They don't make things like this anymore."

Dewi, engrossed in his own exploration, examined a collection of paintings leaning against the wall. His eyes widened as he recognised the brushstrokes and signature of Turner. "Yvonne, look at this," he called, beckoning her over. "These paintings are worth a fortune. They should be in a bank vault, not a storage unit."

They continued their search, stopping to appreciate the artistry in various items. A vintage grandfather clock caught their attention, its steady tick filling the space with a comforting rhythm. Yvonne gazed at the elegant mechanism. Dewi inspected it for hidden compartments that could be exploited for concealment. None were found.

As they progressed, their trained eyes diligently examined every nook and cranny. They scoured the upholstery of a luxurious sofa, and gingerly opened drawers in an antique desk, sifting through old notes and scraps. Nothing stood out or seemed out of place.

Included in the inventory was a vintage gramophone. It evoked memories of the winter afternoons Yvonne had spent at her grandmother's home in Winchester when she and Kim were little; their parents working.

Though captivated by the beauty and historical significance of the items, the DI and Dewi remained focussed on their mission. Hidden amongst these treasures could be evidence crucial to their investigation.

However, after an exhaustive search, they had found no evidence related to the bombing.

"We've covered everything," Yvonne stated, pushing stray hair from her eyes. "There's nothing here that shouldn't be. Nothing that could have been used to manufacture explosives."

"Agreed." Dewi scratched his head. "Looks like he was telling the truth. He's simply storing stuff here in case his home gets burgled again."

"I'd still like to know who the burglar was, and if there is any connection. I think we should push him to provide more detail and examine the files from the original burglary investigation."

"I'll get onto it as soon as we get back." Dewi nodded.

They stopped by the site office, thanking Delyth for her help, before heading back to Newtown CID.

SEVEN O'CLOCK that evening saw the DI still at her desk, long after the others had given up for the day and gone home.

She pored over photographs of the carnage wreaked by the Riverdale bomb. The images had forever captured the brutal aftermath; frozen in time the destruction inflicted upon the van, the mansion gates, and the two men who had lost their lives.

Her fingers traced the contours of the victims' faces, etching their memory deep within her mind. She felt so keenly the weight of the tragedy inflicted on Ted's shattered family, and the emptiness consuming Martin Hawes' wife. Their profound grief clung to her like a heavy shroud, fuelling her need to find them justice.

Someone had orchestrated that horrifying act, crafting a device that tore apart so many lives. The answers lay somewhere within the detail of how the bomb was constructed and the motive behind the attack. Staring at the images, her eyes scanned each minute detail, searching for any hint that could steer her investigation in the right direction. She scoured details of the reconstructed bomb, and compared it to the two duds found afterwards; contemplating the expertise required to assemble such weapons. Each wire and component held a story, a clue that could lead them to whoever made it. She felt the threads were entwined with Rothwell's enigmatic inner circle. Somewhere among those close to him, secrets festered. Someone connected to him had the answers. They had to find out who.

She rose from her desk, glancing at the clock. Tasha would be waiting at home for her. She gathered the photographs, placing them in a folder labelled 'Riverdale Bombing - Evidence.'

On the way out, she paused before the interactive whiteboard. On it, their suspect list, including Rothwell himself. Simon Mason, his erstwhile bass guitarist, had a history of anarchical protests and convictions for criminal damage. Jason Leyland, the cheating best friend. Jeanette Dupont, Rothwell's cheating lover. And Pete Davies, the surviving security guard. The man who appeared to do as little as he could get away with, and who had been terrified of losing his job, should Ted have exposed him. Or was it a stranger? A disgruntled member of the community who felt their voice was not being heard, and this gave them the right to disrupt everybody else's lives in the worst way.

The DI sighed. There was so much more to uncover, but it would have to wait. It was time to step away from the office for another night. Time to go home to the comfort of her partner.

13

A DIABOLICAL PLAN

A lone security guard lifted his peaked-cap to mop his brow with the back of a hand. He had long-since discarded his uniform jacket and his rolled up his shirt sleeves, but still the temperature outside was near unbearable.

A burning sun desiccated the surrounding land; nearly a quarter of the leaves of the estate's grandest sycamore were burned and curling. A storm was long overdue, but showed no sign of coming.

Yvonne watched as a van approached the security hut. It was still some way off as she walked from the direction of the main house. She quickened her pace, even though her energy had drained in the relentless heat. Her legs felt heavy as she walked, like they couldn't be bothered to move.

The guard was now talking to the driver of the van, who held up paperwork for inspection. They were deep in conversation; the vehicle's engine idling away.

Something didn't feel right. Yvonne's gut clenched. Something was wrong. She broke into a run, pushing her legs to go as fast as they could despite the sweat pooling at the base of her back.

She was only feet from the van; holding her hands out towards the guard. "Wait!" she called out. "Get back..."

The explosion burst with a blast of hot air which swept her off her feet. She couldn't see or feel, but felt herself floating, spurred on by the powerful shockwave. Her body hit the ground with a thud. Grit and stones burned into her skin.

"Yvonne? Yvonne?"

"Wh-" She woke covered in sweat, her body shaking.

It took several seconds to come round; to realise she had been dreaming, and Tasha had a gentle arm around her shoulders.

"Are you all right?" The psychologist asked, her forehead creased with concern. "You were having a nightmare and calling out... It must have been terrible?"

The DI shuddered. "It was... I dreamed there was an explosion. I tried to save them..."

Tasha handed Yvonne the glass of water from the bedside cabinet. The cool liquid soothed her throat.

"You don't have to talk about it if you don't want to," Tasha said gently.

Yvonne shook her head. "It was just a dream, though it didn't feel like one. It was so real... like I was there."

Tasha nodded. "Sometimes dreams can be more vivid than reality. Do you want to tell me about it?"

Yvonne took a deep breath and recounted her nightmare, starting from the security guard lifting his cap to mop his brow. As she spoke, the tension in her body lessened. Talking to her partner about the dream had weakened the power and horror of it.

When she finished her story, Tasha sat in silence for a

moment, processing the details. "It sounds like your mind is trying to deal with the traumatic scene you faced at Riverdale. You may have some post-traumatic stress."

"No." The DI shook her head, her hand on the heart still pounding in her chest. "My nightmares could never be compared to the victims' terrible experience."

Her partner nodded. "Still, it must have affected you, Yvonne. I know how deeply you feel things."

The DI leaned her head on Tasha's shoulder, her own rounding as the tension left them. "I felt the blast. I thought I was a goner."

"I'm so glad it wasn't real. I worry about you all the time; the job you do; the danger you face."

"We have to find this bomber, Tasha. I couldn't bear for someone else to lose their life in that way... the sudden awfulness of it. They had no time to call someone or tell their family they loved them." A tear wended its way down the DI's cheek.

"And I know it hurts because you can't go back and save them." The psychologist gave her a squeeze. "But you are doing everything in your power to prevent whoever killed them from doing it again. Your dedication and sense of responsibility are commendable. But, it's important to remember that you can't shoulder the weight of the world alone. It's natural to have these concerns and fears, but it's also crucial to find a balance between duty and your own well-being. Remember, you have a support system. Lean on them, and remember to prioritise your own mental health. If you crumble, who's going to save the world?" Tasha grinned. "I'm teasing, but you get my drift. You're no use to anyone if you become so tired you fall apart."

"I feel like we're getting closer to the answers, though they are still just out of reach. But you are right." Yvonne sighed. "I should rest. I'll need a fresh head tomorrow. We've so much to do."

Tasha plumped her partner's pillow. "Right then, drink some more of that water, and let's get you back off to sleep."

And sleep, she did, because the next thing the DI heard was her morning alarm.

THE NIGHT WAS QUIET, save for an owl hooting occasionally somewhere in the trees.

"You got the money?" The guy in jeans, smelling of sweat, held out his hand.

The man in the dark suit and overcoat glanced at the hand, then at the stubbled, angular face in the half-light, his own countenance creased with disdain. "I want this one to work... It has to go off. I want a big bang."

"Why the change?" Sweaty man raised a brow.

"There are too many questions; cops poking about."

"But a hospital, though?"

The suited man shrugged. "It's full of old people."

"There's a maternity wing..."

"So warn them twenty minutes beforehand."

"How?"

"Figure it out."

"The only way I would know what time it got there would be to take it myself. I can't predict the post."

"So take it there."

"It's easy for you to say."

"You know people."

"I don't take risks."

"Like I say, you'll figure it out. And none of this had better lead back to me."

Sweaty man cleared his throat. "It won't."

"It better not."

"Don't threaten me. I have friends... The kind you wouldn't want to mess with."

"Just make sure it works."

14

BOMBSHELL FROM THE NCA

Yvonne waited for the room to hush, brushing the creases from her black cotton skirt with her hand, and pushing stray hair from her face.

Callum was the first to be seated, signature pencil behind his ear; forehead furrowed in concentration.

"I think I'll get started..." The DI walked over to the whiteboard adorned with photographs and schematics. The room fell into a hushed silence as the detectives waited to hear the latest developments in the case.

She shone her laser pen at the blueprint of Dean Rothwell's mansion. Her strokes were deliberate, pointing to the front gates and the site of the explosion that had rocked the grounds. "We'll start with the bomb at Riverdale," Yvonne began, her voice steady. "It was a powerful blast. They found traces of pulverised concrete amidst the debris. This suggests small concrete blocks had been placed in the package to mask its true contents. These were wrapped in bubble wrap to prevent the tearing of outer packaging."

Dewi's eyes widened. "Of course..."

The DI continued. "A copy of the delivery schedule

carried by Martin Hawes that day stated the parcel was a two-person carry." She rubbed her chin. "If you think about it, the weight alone would guarantee the need for Ted to help carry it into the house. Mr Edwards was not the sort of person to leave a heavy parcel for Rothwell or his friends to move. I believe the bomber knew Ted would assist the delivery driver in carrying it into the hall."

She shifted her focus to the list of suspects, pausing briefly before continuing. "Let's consider Dean Rothwell," Yvonne pointed to his image on the board, her tone thoughtful. "As the owner of Riverdale, and the target of the explosion, was he the victim? Or could he be the perpetrator? We know he had been hoarding valuable possessions at a storage lockup on the outskirts of Welshpool. It's possible he is telling the truth when he states this was because of a previous burglary at Riverdale. But is he? Did he know something big was going to happen at the house? Had he been threatened, and is he withholding that from us? Did he hoard those treasures because he knew his home was at risk from himself or others? Perhaps he intended an insurance scam?"

She continued. "Then we have Simon Mason, another member of the Stoney Bastions, and an anticapitalist activist. We know he has been involved in various protests, and has connections within activist circles. This raises the question of whether he harbours animosity towards Rothwell and his lavish lifestyle? Could Simes have orchestrated an attack like this against his apparent friend and fellow band member? I find it odd that the other musicians do not have a permanent place of their own and appear happy to hang around Riverdale. What is their intention in that regard? Do they have crash pads elsewhere?"

Yvonne pursed her lips, scratching her head in thought.

"Then we have Pete Davies, the surviving security guard," she said, her tone focused. "He would have been at the gates when the device went off, except he delayed the handover with Ted, saying he needed the toilet. Was this a fortuitous coincidence for him? Or something else? There may be more to his involvement than meets the eye. He was adamant that he and Ted got on like a house on fire. But Ted's widow, Rhonda, begs to differ. She has outlined how Ted would complain of Pete being shiftless, and that he was a source of extra strain for her husband because of unreliability. Ted regularly picked up the slack from Pete. Why does Davies give such a different account of things? Ws he afraid Ted would have him fired? Did he act before that could happen, arranging for this device to be delivered? We know he had two personal packages for delivery the same day, which he states were destined for his wife on their anniversary. Again, was this an unfortunate coincidence? Let's keep digging around him."

Yvonne's gaze shifted to the next suspect on the list. "Jason Leyland, Rothwell's best friend, is having an affair with Jeanette Dupont, Rothwell's girlfriend." Her eyes narrowed. "Rothwell is unaware of the affair, but the complicated dynamics between these individuals could be a potential motive. Ted Edwards had seen Dupont and Leyland in a clinch, and they likely knew it. Could that have been a motive for taking him out? After all, if Ted reported to Rothwell what he had seen, both Leyland and Dupont stood to suffer significant personal and financial loss."

"Of course, we could be looking for a stranger unconnected to this group. But, against that, we have two other devices which were never destined to go off. My theory is that this was intentional. It speaks to me of someone wishing to throw suspicion off themselves by making it look like a terrorist act. Except terrorists usually announce what they have done and make demands. Neither of these things happened. I don't know what you guys think, but I still feel that whoever made or ordered these devices is connected to Rothwell and Riverdale."

"I'm with you..." Dewi leaned back in his chair, hands deep in his corduroy pockets. "Because I don't think this was done by a stranger. I have felt from the start the group are hiding things from each other. I believe this story begins and ends with them."

"Thank you, Dewi." Yvonne nodded. "Our next steps are clear, in that case. We should continue investigating each of them, explore their alibis, and delve further into their pasts. Our inquiry will focus on the connections between the burglary; the storage lockup; the explosive devices, and the complex dynamics among these individuals. We are getting closer to the truth. I feel it. But we are not there yet, and God only knows if the perpetrator intends trying again. So, let's redouble our efforts to understand whatever the hell is going on here." She glanced at Callum, their eyes meeting, briefly sharing the silent understanding that the road ahead would be difficult. But they had to uncover the truth behind the explosion that killed Ted Edwards and Martin Hawes.

"Let's get to work," Yvonne said, her gaze steely. "Let's give the families of the victims the justice they deserve."

YVONNE WAS at her desk in Newtown CID. In front of her lay crime scene photographs and maps, as she mulled over the events in the case. The office was alive with activity, as her team made and received phone calls and cross-referenced information as it came in.

Yvonne's phone buzzed, and she glanced at the screen. It was Dave Hanlon of the NCA. She pressed the answer button. "Yvonne speaking," she greeted, hoping he had something for them.

"Yvonne, it's Dave." There was an urgency in his voice. "We have uncovered connections between an indie record label and suspicious overseas transactions. You will want to look at what we found. My feeling is that this is related to your case."

The DI leaned forward, ear pressed tight to the receiver. "Go on?" she said, her tone steady.

Dave took a deep breath; rifling through paperwork. "We've dug deeper into the money trail, Yvonne. This indie label has been withdrawing money from an overseas account, despite no actual record production. I doubt this is a coincidence. We have four large money withdrawals over the last month. The two middle ones were smaller than the first and last."

"Do you think these funds are connected to the acquisition of bomb parts or the payment to the makers of the explosives?" The DI frowned, her mind racing with the implications.

Dave's elevated tone showed his excitement. "We're still piecing it together, but we think we can prove the label is linked to Dean Rothwell and Jeanette Dupont. The identity of the individuals behind this label has been elusive, but we think we've got them on camera making cash withdrawals from a linked account. I'll send you all the relevant information, and, if those monies were for explosive devices, we can coordinate efforts to bring them down. We have identified the group behind the bombs, and the head honcho is Albanian. This group was previously unknown to us. We believe they entered the country illegally and have been hiding out ever since, moving from safe house to safe house. They are making their money through illicit trade of weapons and drugs."

"Wait, if this money really was for explosives, then we potentially have a fourth device? A bomb which could already be out there?"

"And live..."

"Live?" She frowned.

"Yes, if we are right, the larger cash sums were for live devices, and the smaller sums for planned duds. I'm sorry to be the bearer of bad news, but you likely have another explosion on your hands unless we can get Rothwell or Dupont to tell us what is going on. And where the fourth device is?"

"Oh, hell..." The DI ran a hand through her hair, her eyes wide. "Another live bomb is all we need." She got up from her chair. Rothwell and Dupont would have to be picked up as soon as possible. The detonation of another device didn't bear thinking about.

"Thank you, Dave," she said. "We've been preparing for this. The team is ready. Send me the details, and we'll get the couple in for questioning. We'll carry out a raid and pick them up together before they can discuss their stories."

"We'll send you the details right away." Dave ended the call, leaving Yvonne to contemplate the enormity of what she had been told. She called her team together.

15

THE DEVICE FROM HELL

Rothwell glared at Yvonne from across the table, arms folded; his patterned shirt crumpled like he had slept in it. He reeked of cigarettes and alcohol, and appeared not to have shaved for several days. "You could at least have let me shower," he complained, rolling his eyes up to the ceiling. "Who the hell do you lot think you are?"

"Last time I looked, we were the police... with a job to do."

"Where's Jeanie?" He asked, bringing his scowling eyes back to the DI and Dewi.

"She's next door, being interviewed by our colleagues," Dewi answered, folding his arms.

"How long will we be here?" the singer asked. "And why were you in such a hurry? I already told you we know nothing about the explosion at the mansion. We were on tour. This is harassment. You haven't left us alone since we got back. It's exhausting."

"Tell us about the bomb. Who made it? And why did you pay for it?"

"What bomb? You mean the one that killed Ted? Why would I know who made it? And why do you think I paid for it?"

Yvonne rubbed her chin, turning the pages in her notepad. "Let's see now... You own Steeple Vibes, don't you? It says here it is an indie record label started two years ago. Oddly, though, it doesn't appear to have anyone signed to it. Why would you have a record label with no bands or solo artists attached to it?"

"I don't... It's not my label."

"Then whose is it?"

Rothwell shrugged. "I don't know. Never heard of it."

The DI slipped a grainy CCTV still from inside a bank, showing Rothwell talking to a teller. "What do you see in that photo?"

"I dunno. It's someone who looks a bit like me, doing some banking. What of it?" He leaned back in his chair, arms folded again.

"It *is* you, isn't it? Take another look."

He returned his eyes to the photo, elbows on the table. "It could be, I dunno."

"This is you withdrawing twenty-thousand pounds."

He swallowed, his face reddening. "Yeah, it could be."

"We traced that money back to Steeple Vibes."

He stayed silent.

Yvonne could almost hear the wheels turning in his head. "It's your label, isn't it?"

"I might be one of the co-owners of it, yes, but I put my name to many things. I don't remember everything I invest in. If my money was in Steeple Vibes, I'd forgotten about it."

"Really?"

"Really."

"You had forgotten all about it, but you knew the

company contained money, and you could avail yourself of it?"

"Look, what's this about? What are you getting at? So we have a label sitting there in case we discover a new indie band? We need to invest our money somewhere. Ploughing it into an up-and-coming band seems like a sound idea to me, but like I said, I had forgotten all about it."

"How convenient..." The DI leaned back in her chair, tapping her pen against her palm. "What about Jeanie?"

"What about her?" He scowled.

"Is she a co-owner?"

"She might be?"

"Either she is or she isn't. Which is it?"

He sighed. "Yes, she is a co-owner."

"Anyone else have a stake in it?"

"My friend, Jace."

"I see."

"If that has cleared things up for you, can I go now?"

She shook her head. "I'm sorry, we're only getting started. Would you like to have a solicitor present?"

He frowned. "Why?"

"Because we are going to question you about the money you withdrew and the explosion outside of your mansion."

"Wait... You don't think I tried to blow up my house, do you?"

"Did you?"

"No, of course not."

"Perhaps you paid someone else to do it? Are you sure you wouldn't like a solicitor?"

Rothwell ran both hands through his hair. "I don't know. I need to think about it. This is all so sudden. If you are going to accuse me of something, then maybe I need counsel here. Can I have a moment?"

"Sure. We'll leave you with your thoughts for a short while. But know this, we will be back, and this questioning will continue. I strongly suggest you engage a solicitor."

HILARY JONES, fifty-three; a midwife in the maternity suite at Newtown Hospital prepared her patient room for that morning's attendees.

She opened a fresh box of tubes ready for urine tests and checked her watch. It was almost seven-fifteen. The first expectant mother would be with them at half-past.

Her colleague, Mairwen Lloyd, thirty-seven, poked her head around the door. "I thought I would let you know Linda won't be in," she said, referring to their receptionist and admin assistant. "Her daughter is home from school with a sickness bug. Looks like it's just you and me, kiddo."

Hilary sighed, pushing stray hair behind her ear. "Nightmare... We have a few coming in this morning, and I bet the phone will ring off the hook. Also, we'll have to get the door every time someone arrives."

Mairwen grinned. "We'll manage. We always do."

"I've got a woman in for a sweep at half-ten," Hilary advised, referring to the manual manipulation of the cervix used to help kick-start an overdue labour. "The lady is forty-two weeks, and the little one shows no signs of wanting out."

"No problem. I can watch reception while you do the sweep."

"Great." Jones smiled. "The other appointments are routine checks, so they should be in and out without too many problems. We can split the examinations and reception stuff between us, if that's all right with you?"

"Yeah, no problem." Lloyd disappeared again, singing to

herself as she crossed the corridor back to the other patient room.

Ten minutes later, and Hilary's first mum-to-be arrived. The mid-wife began her usual checks on the woman's health, and the progress of her pregnancy, before recording the information in her file.

After measuring the patient's weight and blood pressure, she checked her urine and listened to the baby's heartbeat using a Doppler device. She patiently probed until she could hear the fast-paced rhythm; letting mum listen to the regular and satisfying sound, before measuring her abdomen to determine the baby's growth. "It's coming along exactly as expected." She smiled. "We've no concerns. I know you want a home birth, and I see no reason we can't go ahead with the birth plan. We'll do that when I come to see you at home."

"That's great," the woman's eyes shone. "My husband and I are considering a water birth. What do you think?"

"Perfect." Hilary nodded. "Many women find that water helps them with their pain. We can arrange for the pool to be at your home, nearer the time."

Hilary discussed breastfeeding, birth preparations, and pain management, and answered the woman's questions.

Finally, they were done. And the midwife rose to show the lady out. "I'll see you in a month, Margaret, unless a problem arises in the meantime."

Mairwen poked her head around the door again. "Can you let the postman in? He's got a parcel for us, and my next patient is waiting." She screwed her nose up. "Sorry to put this on you. It's just that my lady has to catch a bus in twenty minutes."

"Sure, I've got fifteen minutes until my lady comes in for the sweep. I'll sort the postman."

Mairwen grinned, raising a brow. "Oh, aye?"

Hilary laughed. "You know what I mean," she pulled a face, before wandering down the corridor to let him in.

He was standing outside of the door, waiting patiently, a broad smile on his rugged, stubbled features. "I might need to take it in for you," he advised. "It's quite heavy."

Behind him, Hilary spied her next patient. She was ten minutes early. The midwife shrugged at the postman. "Yes, I'm sorry, we have no reception. Can you set the parcel down over there? Below the office window? Our admin lass can deal with it tomorrow when she returns. We are run off our feet here, as always."

He nodded. "Sure... no problem." He did as he was told, setting the package down on the corridor floor and whistling as he left. He gave Hilary a wave, but she was already leading the heavily pregnant young woman and her mother towards the patient room and didn't see it.

Sarah Edwards rubbed her oversized bump with both hands. Her amble along the corridor was half shuffle; half waddle.

Rhonda looked on with pride, her arm through her daughter's as she helped her follow their midwife. "Your dad would be so excited," she whispered. "Ted would be over the moon right now."

16

TENTERHOOKS

Jeanie Dupont sat with her long legs crossed and her chair pushed farther back from the table as though she had no wish to engage. As Yvonne entered the room, the former model returned her compact and mirror to the handbag hanging from her chair. She pressed her lips together, gazing at her fingernails.

The DI flicked Dewi a glance before setting her level gaze back on the woman opposite. According to Callum and Dai, Jeanie had refused a solicitor, saying she didn't need one as she had done nothing wrong. "Hello, Jeanie." She leaned forward, elbows on her paperwork.

Dupont sighed, dragging her eyes away from her fingernails and back to Yvonne. "Why am I still here?" she asked, folding her arms. "I've said all I want to say. You can't keep me... I'm not under arrest."

"That could change."

Jeanie's eyes narrowed. "What do you mean?"

"We have information which could result in serious charges being brought against you. That is why my colleagues suggested you engage a solicitor. We have important questions to put to you, Ms Dupont, and I would like direct and honest answers."

The woman shifted in her seat.

"Jeanette, we understand you have a share in Steeple Vibes, an indie record label. Am I right?"

Jeanie shrugged. "What of it if I do?"

"We believe money from that company was used to purchase items from an Albanian criminal group who are operating in our country illegally."

"What items?"

"Improvised explosive devices."

Dupont lowered her eyes, clearing her throat. Her chest and neck reddened.

"Jeanie, this is really important. Lives are at stake. What do you know of these bombs?"

Dupont maintained her defensive posture, arms still folded as she stared at Yvonne. Her expression remained guarded, but a flicker of concern passed over her eyes. Her lips pursed, though she narrowed gaze in defiance. "I already told you, I know nothing about any items or bombs, and I wouldn't have a clue what they look like. I simply own shares in record companies... It's not a crime to invest."

Yvonne leaned forward, her voice laden with urgency. "Jeanie, listen to me. We know there is a fourth bomb, and it's crucial we find it. We believe it will go off in a public place. More people will die. Do you hear me, Jeanie? More people like Ted. We need to know where it is... Where it has been sent. If you have any information, please tell us now."

Dupont's eyes darted around the room, her discomfort clear. She bit her lower lip, torn by an internal struggle, though she still said nothing.

Yvonne paused for a moment, her eyes fixed on the woman's face. She took a deep breath before speaking, her tone stern and resolute. "Jeanie, as I told you last time, we know about your affair with Jason Leyland, your partner's best friend. I'm sure you wouldn't want Dean getting wind of it?"

Her face paled, eyes widening in fear. She clenched her fists, her voice trembling as she responded. "You wouldn't..."

"It could slip out. We are a large team. Tongues become loose after a beer or two."

Dupont shifted uncomfortably in her seat, wringing her hands and biting her lip. "What else do you want to know? I've told you everything I can."

"Yourself and Rothwell planned the Riverdale bombing, didn't you? You planned it together. You wanted Ted out of the way because he knew too much. And Dean, your partner, went along with it. The question is why? Why did Dean go along with it? What was in it for him? Or did you simply work on him until he gave in to something he had no reason for?"

"It was his bloody idea!" Jeanie blurted. "He bloody started this whole thing... Dean got us into this ruddy mess in the first place."

"Oh, did he?" Yvonne leaned back in her chair, suppressing a satisfied grin. "You had better tell us everything you know."

"Fine..." Jeanie put her head in her hands, her voice barely above a whisper. "I knew of the bomb at Riverdale. I knew of Dean's plan. But it wasn't what you think... It was never meant to hurt anyone."

"Then what was the reason for it?"

"Insurance."

"You needed the money?" Yvonne frowned. This was hard to believe.

"We wanted to rebuild and partially remodel the entrance hall and reception rooms. The work we wanted would have cost nearly a quarter of a million. We have money, but not nearly enough for that. The package should have been left in the hallway below the stairs. We were away, and security staff would not usually be inside the property for much of the day. The explosion should have happened when no-one was around. But it was volatile, you see... It should have been kept cool. And that day was scorching. Bloody typical... The chemicals should have been in a fridge at that temperature. That is what the bomb makers told Dean."

"What about the devices sent to the court and the supermarket?"

"Look, those explosives were never meant to go off. They were only supposed to take attention away from Riverdale and us. To make it look like some random lunatic had a grievance against society. That is it. That is everything. I swear, I do not know of any other device. As far as I know, there are no other bombs. Dean and I agreed enough was enough, and it had already gone too far. He promised me there would be no more."

"It has gone too far... Two people are dead. You could go away for a very long time. And you would never come out if another device goes off in a public place."

"I swear to God, I know of no other device." Jeanie's eyes were wide; pleading. "If I did, I would tell you."

Finally, they were getting somewhere. Even if Dupont knew nothing of the fourth bomb, Rothwell almost certainly did. They now had exactly what they needed to apply pressure on him. Despite a visceral dislike of the methods of used by the couple, Yvonne maintained her professional composure. "Thank you for finally being honest, Jeanie. I strongly urge you to avail yourself of a solicitor as soon as you can."

Rothwell's lips tightened, and he glanced away momentarily before meeting Yvonne's gaze again. "Look, I invested my money in Steeple Vibes, but I have no control over how it's managed or what they do with the funds. I trusted the people running the label."

Yvonne nodded, acknowledging his statement. She would play along for the moment. "I understand... Did you notice any unusual transactions? Or dealings that could be linked to illegal purchases?"

His gaze shifted as he cleared his throat. "Look, I only glanced at the financial reports and let others worry about the details. I'm always so busy with other things. Everything seemed legitimate to me. I don't scrutinise every transaction. Why would I? Maybe someone was misusing the funds without my knowledge?"

"Who?"

He shrugged.

"Your friend Jason?"

"Maybe?"

Yvonne leaned in, her gaze steely; voice firm. "You need to be honest with us, Dean. If you have information, give it to us now if you want to prevent further harm. Did anyone associated with Steeple Vibes show any interest in acquiring explosives?" She watched his face intently, scrutinising every twitch of his facial muscles. The man was evidently uncomfortable.

Rothwell hesitated. His bulging eyes shifted as he flicked them side-to-side, thinking of what to say, and how much he should divulge. "There was this one person... Max. He's a producer at the label, and always seemed a bit off, but I didn't suspect him of anything like this. He has connections, though. Maybe he's involved."

"Max?" She raised an eyebrow, exaggerating the jotting down of the name in her notes.

"Max Leverson. He's in charge of the day-to-day running of the business."

"The running of a label with no artists?"

"It will have artists in the future." Rothwell glowered. "These things take time."

"And this Max person... He would need explosives? Why?" she asked, her brow still raised.

"I dunno. You should ask him."

"Where would I find him?"

Rothwell shrugged.

"You see..." The DI continued. "I don't think this Max Leverson exists. He doesn't, does he? You made him up, just like you continue to make up stories to cover your backside. The problem with telling tall tales is you have to tell bigger and bigger ones to keep the whole thing going. And then you have to remember all the stories you have told so they don't seem full of holes. Like the ones you're telling me now."

He glared at her. "How would you know? You know nothing of my world."

"Ain't that the truth?" She sighed. "Let me put it a different way, Mr Rothwell. I believe you have been lying to me all the way along. I get it... A man died. A man who had served you loyally, and whom you cared about. It wasn't meant to happen, but it did, and you caused it. And you felt it necessary to hide that fact from the world and us, didn't you?"

HILARY JONES, the Newtown mid-wife, led the heavily pregnant Sarah Edwards and her mother, Rhonda, into the patient room.

Rhonda clenched her daughter's hand to comfort and support while Sarah described her symptoms to the midwife.

Hilary helped the young woman lie on the bed, explaining about Braxton Hicks contractions to ease her anxiety. "Alright, Sarah," she said. "Let's see how you and your little one are doing before we start with the sweep."

Hilary began the examination, carefully assessing Sarah's blood pressure and testing her urine sample. Sarah explained the contractions had become more frequent in the past few days. Concerned, Hilary examined Sarah's cervix. She checked for signs of progression and assessed whether the sweep was still needed.

As Hilary carried out the procedure, Sarah winced.

Rhonda stood beside her daughter, her face a mixture of concern and nervousness. She held her breath as Hilary finished the examination.

Sarah's eyes widened as a surge of discomfort washed over her. She grasped Hilary's arm, her voice urgent. "Something's happening... That contraction hurt." She screwed her eyes up as another wave came up and over her belly.

Realising Sarah was going into labour sooner than they had expected, Hilary sprang into action. "Don't worry, Sarah. We're ready for this. Breath with me," she instructed, reaching for her pager to call for immediate help from Mairwen. She then began breathing with the young woman while preparing pain medication.

Within moments, Mairwen Lloyd, the second midwife, joined them.

"She needs pain relief. I think she's going to have the baby." Hilary advised, frowning in concentration.

Mairwen took her to one side. "It's hot, and it's going to get hotter, I'm afraid. The air conditioning is out."

Hilary sighed. "It's all happening today, isn't it? No matter... We just have to get on with it."

Sarah's contractions intensified, and her waters broke, signalling the onset of active labour.

Hilary and Mairwen prepared their equipment, making sure everything was ready for imminent delivery.

Rhonda held Sarah's hand, offering words of encouragement, as tears welled in her eyes.

Hilary positioned herself at Sarah's side, guiding her through each contraction, coaching her to breathe and relax. Mairwen stood ready to assist and ensure the well-being of both mother and baby. They gave off an aura of competence and calm; their years of experience and expertise reassuring the mum-to-be and her mother.

Time blurred as the labour progressed. The room filled with the sounds of Sarah's deep breathing, the rhythmic beeping of the foetal monitor, and the reassuring voices of the mid-wives.

Rhonda stood patiently at her daughter's side, reminding herself every so often not to squeeze her hand too tightly.

Along the corridor sat a lone package, its ominous contents unknown to the four women working hard to bring new life into the world.

Ted's grandchild was on the way, unaware of the nightmare looming down the hall.

17

TURNING THE SCREWS

"No." Rothwell scowled.

"Didn't you?" Yvonne persisted.

"I don't know what you are talking about," he hissed, spittle hitting the desk in front of him.

"That's not what Jeanie told me..."

"What do you mean?" She had his full attention, and there was a question behind the eyes. He was becoming unsure of himself.

"Your partner, Jeanette Dupont, has confessed everything to us."

"I don't believe you." He shook his head. "There is nothing to confess."

"We know you planned the destruction of your entrance hall and reception rooms."

"What?"

"We know you wanted the insurance money because the restructuring you desired was going to set you back a quarter of a million."

He opened his mouth and closed it again, eyes like wheels.

"You didn't mean to kill Ted Edwards, we know that. He was your hardest working; most reliable employee. He had served you faithfully for many years. But it all went wrong, didn't it? Neither you nor the bomb-maker planned for a June temperature as intense as the one that day. Am I right? The Albanian mob who made the device warned you about heat. They told you to make sure the package was kept cool, didn't they?"

He remained silent, but his eyes remained round and his chest heaved.

"It would have been okay if they could have gotten it into your marble hall, right? It was far cooler in there than in Martin Hawes' hot van. The vehicle would have been like an oven in that heat."

"I-" Again, he stopped himself.

"That van blew up in the burning sun, its sides giving way like butter in the explosion. And two men... two men beloved by their families were blasted from the world... Just like that. Your wants. Your needs. Your diabolical plan, and that volatile bomb. Those men needlessly lost their lives."

He gazed at the table in front of him, head bowed.

"You know you will go away for a long time, right?"

Silence.

"And we know there's another device, Dean. We know it will go off, showing how far you were you willing to go to cover your tracks. Hellish deeds are like false narratives. You dig yourself deeper and deeper, trying to keep a lid on it all. It never ends well, Rothwell. And it won't end well for you if this last bomb goes off. You harm any more people and you will go away and never come out. If you do not tell us where the fourth device is, there will be no mitigating circumstances at court. If anyone dies this time, you won't be looking at manslaughter, like you might face for Ted and

Martin's death... You'll be looking at murder. You could go away for good."

He looked up from the table, chewing the inside of his cheek. "I don't want anyone else to get hurt," he said, shaking his head. "I didn't want any of this..."

"Then tell us where to find the last package, Dean. Tell us before anyone else gets hurt."

"Push," Hilary instructed, drawing the word out for emphasis. "Come on, now, push, Sarah, you can do it." Sweat dripped from the midwife's forehead and soaked the back of her scrubs.

The young woman was also drenched in perspiration as she took rapid breaths, pushing with the contractions.

Mairwen mopped her brow. She cast a sideways glance at Hilary. "This heat..."

Rhonda used a damp flannel to cool her daughter's forehead.

"Come on now, push... This time, Sarah. This time... We have the head, Sarah, you are doing fantastic. One more push. Go for it."

Sarah pushed hard one final time, and her little one came out in a wet whoosh, ejecting easily now the head was through.

Hilary cut the cord while Mairwen took the baby to swab it down and check its vital signs.

Cries from the newborn had them all laughing and crying at once. Little Ted, named after his lately deceased grandfather, had finally entered the world. His moans of complaint at the drama of it all were like music to his mother and grandmother.

Mairwen placed the baby on Sarah's chest, where his cries eased away, replaced by gurgles.

Sarah kissed his tiny head, softly squeezing him to her. "Welcome to the world, my little man." She smiled through tears of happiness. "We've been waiting for you."

18

A TERRIFYING RACE AGAINST TIME

"Come on, Dean. Tell us where the last bomb is. Lives are depending on it." Yvonne leaned towards him, her voice low. "The game is up. You know it is. Let it out... Please?"

Rothwell ran both hands through his hair, his face contorting with angst. "I didn't want this," he blurted. "I didn't want any of it."

"Just tell us where the package has been sent."

"It's gone to the hospital." He checked his watch. "It should have arrived already."

"Which hospital?" The DI frowned, heart racing. "Why a bloody hospital, of all places?"

"Newtown... It's at Newtown hospital. The maternity wing..."

"Oh, God..." The DI grabbed her mobile, turning to her DS. "Dewi, can you shoot upstairs to the DCI, and let him know what's happening? Ask him to get onto the bomb squad right away."

She used her mobile to ring the CID main office. "Dai?

Please telephone Newtown Hospital and ask them not to open any packages. I repeat, they must not open any packages. Explain to them the need to evacuate the hospital without delay. Tell them if they have received any parcels, they need to use doors well away from them."

"Right you are." He hung up.

She arrested Rothwell on suspicion of manslaughter and attempted murder; then requested two constables take him to the cells before arresting Jeanette Dupont.

The DI checked her watch, praying the hospital had been contacted in time. Heart thumping hard inside her chest, she grabbed her jacket from the back of the chair and ran for the car park.

THE LANE LEADING to the Newtown hospital was a frenzy of activity. The road was cordoned off as people and beds were led to safety.

Yvonne had been at the scene for twenty minutes by the time Chris Llewelyn, the DCI, joined her.

"What do we know?" he asked as he caught up with her at the edge of the cordon.

"Only one package arrived for maternity today. It was left in the corridor beside their admin office. Thank God their receptionist was not in, and the midwives were too busy this morning to open it. There is a problem though, sir. The air conditioning isn't working on the wing, and the day is really hotting up. I'm told the air is stifling inside, and the bomb inside the parcel is heat sensitive. We're moving everybody as far back as possible and I understand the bomb squad is on its way?"

"It is." He nodded. "I made sure of that, myself."

"Thank you, Chris. Let's pray they get here in time. I haven't spoken with the midwives yet, but a baby was born this morning. I was about to go check on them."

"Sounds like you are on top of things," Llewelyn nodded. "I hear you have Dean Rothwell in custody? The Stoney Bastions were one of my favourite bands growing up." He raised a brow, a twinkle in his eyes. "You can't arrest people for making music you don't like, you know..."

She grinned despite herself and the tense situation. "Very funny..." She pulled a face. "Rothwell won't be making any music for a while."

The DCI scratched his head, his gaze wandering up the hill to where patients were still being pushed or helped down the lane. "I would never have thought this of him. My childhood beliefs have been shattered."

Yvonne pursed her lips. "If bomb squad do not arrive soon, there could be a lot more shattered than your boyhood notions."

Llewelyn checked his watch. "At least the fire service is here, and it looks like everybody is out of the building now."

"Thank goodness." She checked her watch, the sun bearing down on them. "The trouble is, until the army has assessed the power of this device, we do not know how big the blast could be." She glanced at the houses to their left, going up the lane. "I think those dwellings should be evacuated."

"I'll speak to uniform," he agreed. "We should get everyone out of there as soon as possible." He left her side to approach two officers on the main road.

In the distance, sirens could be heard approaching. Sergeant Denholm's unit was on its way.

THE WAILING of sirens grew louder as the army logistics corps raced towards Newtown Hospital

Upon their arrival, Denholm swiftly gathered his gear, and began donning his protective bomb suit, helped by a colleague.

The DI could see the determination on his expressive face, confirming the gravity of the situation and the danger they were in. The sweltering heat would only add to the discomfort in that heavy armour, and the danger from the device inside. But the sergeant's eyes remained focussed on the monitor screen in front of him.

Guiding the robot with cameras and sensors, Denholm manoeuvred it towards the package in the maternity corridor. The tension was palpable as everyone held their breath, eyes fixed on him as he assessed the live feed from the roving arm.

The hospital, once bustling with life, was now eerily empty. All patients and staff had been successfully evacuated, but the threat loomed over the place where they worked and sought care.

Yvonne bit her lip, knowing inside the hospital, a broken air-conditioning could easily spell disaster. She shifted the weight between her feet.

Uniformed officers made their way up the lane, knocking on doors and removing shocked residents from their houses.

The DI returned her eyes to Denholm, knowing as the minutes ticked away, the weight of the situation pressed upon his shoulders more than anyone else's.

Though the sergeant's brow dripped, his gloved hand remained controlled as he manoeuvred the robotic device closer to the package. Every movement was deliberate, every decision weighed against potential consequences.

The robot scanned the parcel, capturing detailed images, and relaying crucial information back to Denholm and his team. The tension was near unbearable as they waited.

Finally, the robot transmitted images confirming a live bomb, and the crowd fell into a hushed silence as Denholm steeled himself for work ahead. Having seen how the device was put together, he would now dismantle it manually.

The DI watched as his larger-than-life form began the long walk into the hospital through its sliding doors.

Seconds stretched into agonising minutes as they waited for him to navigate the web of wires and mechanisms. Yvonne could picture beads of sweat as they trickled down his forehead and off the end of his nose. Could imagine the grimace of intense concentration as he carefully completed his work. The DI felt nauseous.

Finally, a shout went up from an army colleague, confirming Denholm had disarmed the bomb, rendering it inert. The tension that had gripped them dissolved into floods of overwhelming gratitude. Applause erupted from those watching, mingled with tears of relief.

Yvonne exhaled, her stomach sore from the time her muscles had been clenched.

Denholm came out from the hospital and removed his helmet, hair plastered to his head with sweat; on his face a mix of exhaustion and exhilaration. He glanced around, meeting the eyes of relieved onlookers. The weight of the responsibility he carried had dissipated, replaced by a profound sense of satisfaction.

Hospital patients and staff had only to wait for the

remnants of the bomb to be removed before reentering the hospital and carrying on with their lives.

The DI climbed the lane into the tiny car park at the front of the building, following the DCI as he met with staff to confirm they could soon go inside.

19

NEW BEGINNINGS

Yvonne located the midwives who had delivered a baby while oblivious to a bomb down the hall. She approached Hilary and Mairwen as they wheeled the new mum up the ramp and back into the maternity building; regarding them with a sense of relief and genuine concern. The harrowing experience they had endured weighed heavily on her, and she wanted to offer comfort amidst the chaos.

She waited as they settled in before announcing her presence. "DI Giles, Newtown Police. I came to check on you. I know how terrifying it must have been for you out there while the bomb was deactivated," she said, her eyes falling on the young mum and child. "I am so glad you and the baby are well."

Hilary and Mairwen exchanged glances, their faces etched with exhaustion. They had been through a tremendous ordeal, hearts heavy with concern for the safety of the mother and her newborn child.

"DI Giles," Hilary replied, her voice trembling. "Sarah and Ted did really well, didn't you?" She inclined her head, a smile belying the tremulous hand holding the bedhead.

Mairwen agreed, hand on her chest, still heaving from the adrenaline. "It was a scary situation. We're just grateful the bomb was deactivated."

Yvonne nodded, her eyes soft with empathy. "Thank God for people like Sergeant Denholm and his team. Their actions saved lives today." She turned to the new mum. "May I ask, are you Sarah Edwards?"

The girl nodded, eyes wide, silently wondering how the DI knew who she was.

Rhonda ran down the corridor, bottles of cold drinking water in her arms. "Sorry about the delay. I got these from officers outside. I thought we could all use some." Her gaze met Yvonne's. "DI Giles, meet Ted Junior... My Ted's new grandson."

A broad smile spread over Yvonne's face. "Little Ted..." Her eyes sparkled. "Well, hello there, tiny man. It's lovely to meet you..." Her mind wandered for a moment, reflecting on the delicate cycle of life. The world always came full circle in its own peculiar way. While one life had been stolen by violence, another had emerged, bringing hope and a sense of continuity to those left behind. This filled her with a sense of justice as she refocused her attention on the young mother and her newborn. "He's a beautiful baby," she said, her voice tender. "And Ted... Such a fitting name. I hope his life will be filled with love, happiness, and the knowledge of his grandfather. I'm sure his granddad is smiling down right now, feeling proud."

Sarah looked up at the DI, tears and hope glistened in her eyes. The presence of little Ted offered the family a ray of light in what had been several weeks of darkness. "Thank you, DI Giles," she whispered. "It means a lot to hear that."

Yvonne nodded. "Take your time, get to know your little one, and cherish every moment. If there is anything you need, please do not hesitate to reach out to us. We're here to help support you." She took Rhonda to one side. "We have Ted's killer in custody. Your husband's death was unintentional, but the man whose reckless actions caused your loss will go away for a considerable time."

"Thank God..." Rhonda's eyes travelled to her grandson. "He won't be able to hurt anyone else."

"That's right, he won't, and I rather think Pete Davies will be looking for alternative employment. Good luck with everything, Rhonda... Enjoy your new grandson." With those words, Yvonne stepped away, allowing the new mother and grandmother to immerse themselves in the joy of their newborn.

As she left through the hospital corridor, she was left with mixed emotions. Sad they had lost a member of their family, but glad they had a new life to sustain them. They would be all right. That was the main thing.

BACK IN CID, Dewi made them all a brew, handing around mugs of tea and packets of digestives.

The DCI joined them, taking off his tie and undoing his top button. "I wanted to thank you all. That was good work today, well done. How did you get Rothwell to confess? I'm assuming you didn't bring out the thumbscrews?" He grinned. "Though under the circumstances, I couldn't have blamed you if you did."

Yvonne smiled back. "Believe me, at one point I was tempted... I think the rack might have been more my choice."

"Seriously, though," Llewelyn continued. "I know how hard you worked on this case. Hanlon and Taylor were in touch earlier. They said you helped them get their teeth into an Albanian gang who are new to the country. They still are rounding them up as we speak, which I know will save countless lives going forward. That alone is a reason for us to celebrate the work we do. I know it wasn't easy, but you have produced results again, and there is a brand new baby who likely owes its life to this team. I know I have the best officers on the force, thank you... All of you."

20

A WEDDING IN THE OFFING

The summer evening cast a warm glow over Newtown's Park Street, as Yvonne and Tasha ambled towards the Greek restaurant opposite Dolerw Park.

The soft music of bouzouki strings floated in the air, mingling with the chatter of diners, creating an atmosphere befitting a celebration.

As they entered, the aromatic scent of grilled meats, roasted vegetables, and freshly baked bread teased their nostrils. Yvonne hadn't realised how hungry she was.

Flickering candles on their table cast a gentle light, adding an intimate touch to the surroundings. The walls were adorned with photographs of picturesque Greek islands, whisking them off to distant shores.

A smiling waiter seated them at a corner table, offering the menu of mouth-watering dishes. Yvonne's gaze lingered over the choices while her partner scoured the wine list.

"Shall we try the Agiorgitiko?" Tasha asked, her head cocked. "It's a red wine from Nemea, with rich flavours and velvety texture."

Yvonne glanced at the description and nodded. "Sounds perfect. Let's go with that." She narrowed her eyes at her partner. "What's going on?"

Tasha laughed as the waiter returned, pouring the deep crimson liquid into their glasses. The wine's aroma filled the air with the scent of blackberry and a touch of spice.

Yvonne took a sip. It felt smooth and robust as she rolled it around her tongue. "Come on... You're up to something, I know it..."

Tasha grinned. "Patience is a virtue..."

As the waiter brought their chosen Greek delicacies—spanakopita, dolmades, and moussaka—the conversation flowed effortlessly between the two, though the psychologist had still not answered the DI's question.

As they finished their main course, Tasha's eyes sparkled with anticipation as she cleared her throat. She swallowed another mouthful of wine. "Yvonne," she began, gently squeezing her partner's hand, "I hope you don't mind, but I booked the church for our wedding in October."

Surprise flickered across Yvonne's face, her mind processing the idea of taking the last step towards matrimony. She was happy with their relationship, but the thought of a wedding brought anxiety. What if it ruined what they had? The loss she had suffered in the past still haunted her. The death of her husband in a horrific air accident. She shuddered, shaking off the notion. It wasn't marriage that caused his loss. But would this last step be tempting fate?

A look of doubt clouded Tasha's features. "I'm sorry. Was I wrong to go ahead?"

Yvonne smiled, shaking her head. "My darling Tasha, I honestly do not know what I would do without you in my life. I haven't made it easy for you, and I know I have caused you to worry about the anxiety I sometimes feel. But I can tell you this, I love you. And I want to spend the rest of my life with you. So, no... You were not wrong to go ahead. I am glad you booked it. It will stop me from prevaricating." She raised her glass. "To us."

Relief washed over Tasha, her eyes sparkling. She reached across the table, gently brushing her fingers against Yvonne's cheek. "I'm so glad, Yvonne. I love you more than words. And I'll do everything I can to make our day special." She raised her wine. "To us."

They clinked their glasses together, sealing the commitment.

Details of the wedding could be sorted in due course. Yvonne envisioned a quiet affair, knowing it might be a bone of contention with her smiling partner. But, for now, she was content to relish the moment, knowing they were finally forging ahead with their plans.

Amidst the contented buzz of the restaurant, Tasha raised her glass again. "And congratulations on solving another case, Yvonne. The dedication of you and your team never ceases to amaze me."

"Oh, go on with you..." The DI grinned. "You work with the cream of the bunch down in the Big Smoke. We're small fry compared to that."

"Ah, you'd be surprised." Tasha pursed her lips. "By the way," she added. "I was thinking... after the wedding... We might get a new kitchen; open up the space a bit. It can get ever so cramped when I'm cooking up a storm. Of course, it might require some remodelling of the house."

Yvonne grimaced. "Just don't go bombing the place for the insurance money." She laughed.

A look of confusion clouded the psychologist's face. "What?"

"It's what our killer intended to do with his mansion."

"Oh, I see." Tasha palmed her forehead. "Trust me to put my foot in it."

Yvonne's smile widened, her heart filled with pride and gratitude for having Tasha not only as a partner but also as her biggest supporter. "You could never actually put your foot in anything. You are fabulous, even when you don't know you are."

"Well, that's a relief." Tasha grinned. "I don't want a divorce before we're even married."

They continued with food, their laughter blending with the melodic strains of background music.

As they finished their meal, Yvonne looked forward to this future shared with her soulmate.

AFTERWORD

Mailing list: You can join my emailing list here : AnnamarieMorgan.com

Facebook page: AnnamarieMorganAuthor

You might also like to read the other books in the series:
Book 1: Death Master:

After months of mental and physical therapy, Yvonne Giles, an Oxford DI, is back at work and that's just how she likes it. So when she's asked to hunt the serial killer responsible for taking apart young women, the DI jumps at the chance but hides the fact she is suffering debilitating flashbacks. She is told to work with Tasha Phillips, an in-her-face, criminal psychologist. The DI is not enamoured with the idea. Tasha has a lot to prove. Yvonne has a lot to get over. A tentative link with a 20 year-old cold case brings them closer to the truth but events then take a horrifyingly personal turn.

Book 2: You Will Die

After apprehending an Oxford Serial Killer, and almost losing her life in the process, DI Yvonne Giles has left England for a quieter life in rural Wales. Her peace is shattered when she is asked to hunt a priest-killing psychopath, who taunts the police with messages inscribed on the corpses. Yvonne requests the help of Dr. Tasha Phillips, a psychologist and friend, to aid in the hunt. But the killer is one step ahead and the ultimatum, he sets them, could leave everyone devastated.

Book 3: Total Wipeout

A whole family is wiped out with a shotgun. At first glance, it's an open-and-shut case. The dad did it, then killed himself. The deaths follow at least two similar family wipeouts – attributed to the financial crash.

So why doesn't that sit right with Detective Inspector Yvonne Giles? And why has a rape occurred in the area, in the weeks preceding each family's demise? Her seniors do not believe there are questions to answer. DI Giles must therefore risk everything, in a high-stakes investigation of a mysterious masonic ring and players in high finance.

Can she find the answers, before the next innocent family is wiped out?

Book 4: Deep Cut

In a tiny hamlet in North Wales, a female recruit is murdered whilst on Christmas home leave. Detective Inspector Yvonne Giles is asked to cut short her own leave, to investigate. Why was the young soldier killed? And is her death related to several alleged suicides at her army base? DI Giles this it is, and that someone powerful has a dark secret they will do anything to hide.

Book 5: The Pusher

Young men are turning up dead on the banks of the River Severn. Some of them have been missing for days or even weeks. The only thing the police can be sure of, is that the men have drowned. Rumours abound that a mythical serial killer has turned his attention from the Manchester canal to the waterways of Mid-Wales. And now one of CID's own is missing. A brand new recruit with everything to live for. DI Giles must find him before it's too late.

Book 6: Gone

Children are going missing. They are not heard from again until sinister requests for cryptocurrency go viral. The public must pay or the children die. For lead detective Yvonne Giles, the case is complicated enough. And then the unthinkable happens...

Book 7: Bone Dancer

A serial killer is murdering women, threading their bones back together, and leaving them for police to find. Detective Inspector Yvonne Giles must find him before more innocent victims die. Problem is, the killer wants her and will do anything he can to get her. Unaware that she, herself, is is a target, DI Giles risks everything to catch him.

Book 8: Blood Lost

A young man comes home to find his whole family missing. Half-eaten breakfasts and blood spatter on the lounge wall are the only clues to what happened...

Book 9: Angel of Death

The peace of the Mid-Wales countryside is shattered, when a female eco-warrior is found crucified in a public wood. At first, it would appear a simple case of finding which of the woman's enemies had had her killed. But DI Yvonne Giles has no idea how bad things are going to get. As the body count rises, she will need all of her instincts, and the skills of those closest to her, to stop the murderous rampage of the Angel of Death.

Book 10: Death in the Air

Several fatal air collisions have occurred within a few months in rural Wales. According to the local Air Accidents Investigation Branch (AAIB) inspector, it's a coincidence. Clusters happen. Except, this cluster is different. DI Yvonne Giles suspects it when she hears some of the witness statements but, when an AAIB inspector is found dead under a bridge, she knows it.

Something is way off. Yvonne is determined to get to the bottom of the mystery, but exactly how far down the treacherous rabbit hole is she prepared to go?

Book 11: Death in the Mist

The morning after a viscous sea-mist covers the seaside town of Aberystwyth, a young student lies brutalised within one hundred yards of the castle ruins.

DI Yvonne Giles' reputation precedes her. Having successfully captured more serial killers than some detectives have caught colds, she is seconded to head the murder investigation team, and hunt down the young woman's killer.

What she doesn't know, is this is only the beginning...

Book 12: Death under Hypnosis

When the secretive and mysterious Sheila Winters approaches Yvonne Giles and tells her that she murdered someone thirty years before, she has the DI's immediate attention.

Things get even more strange when Sheila states:

She doesn't know who.

She doesn't know where.

She doesn't know why.

Book 13: Fatal Turn

A seasoned hiker goes missing from the Dolfor Moors after recording a social media video describing a narrow cave he intends to explore. A tragic accident? Nothing to see here, until a team of cavers disappear on a coastal potholing expedition, setting off a string of events that has DI Giles tearing her hair out. What, or who is the thread that ties this series of disappearances together?

A serial killer, thriller murder-mystery set in Wales.

Book 14: The Edinburgh Murders

A newly-retired detective from the Met is murdered in a murky alley in Edinburgh, a sinister calling card left with the body.

The dead man had been a close friend of psychologist Tasha Phillips, giving her her first gig with the Met decades before.

Tasha begs DI Yvonne Giles to aid the Scottish police in solving the case.

In unfamiliar territory, and with a ruthless killer haunting the streets, the DI plunges herself into one of the darkest, most terrifying cases of her career. Who exactly is The Poet?

Book 15: A Picture of Murder

Men are being thrown to their deaths in rural Wales.

At first glance, the murders appear unconnected until DI Giles uncovers potential links with a cold case from the turn of the Millennium.

Someone is eliminating the witnesses to a double murder.

DI Giles and her team must find the perpetrator before all the witnesses are dead.

Book 16: The Wilderness Murders

People are disappearing from remote locations.

Abandoned cars, neatly piled belongings, and bizarre last photographs, are the only clues for what happened to them.

Did they run away? Or, as DI Giles suspects, have they fallen prey to a serial killer who is taunting police with the heinous pieces of a puzzle they must solve if they are to stop the wilderness murderer.

Book 17: The Bunker Murders

A murder victim found in a shallow grave has DI Yvonne Giles and her team on the hunt for both the killer and a motive for the well-loved man's demise.

Yvonne cannot help feeling the killing is linked to a string of female disappearances stretching back nearly two decades.

Someone has all the answers, and the DI will stop at nothing to find them and get to the bottom of this perplexing mystery.

Book 18: The Garthmyl Murders

A missing brother and friends with dark secrets have DI Giles turning circles after a body is found face-down in the pond of a local landmark.

Stymied by a wall of silence and superstition, Yvonne and her team must dig deeper than ever if they are to crack this impossible case.

Who, or what, is responsible for the Garthmyl murders?

Book 19: The Signature

When a young woman is found dead inside a rubbish dumpster after a night out, police chiefs are quick to label it a tragic accident. But as more bodies surface, Detective Inspector Yvonne Giles is convinced a cold-blooded murderer is on the loose. She believes the perpetrator is devious and elusive, disabling CCTV cameras in the area, and leaving them with little to go on. With time running out, Giles and her team must race against the clock to catch the killer or killers before they strike again.

Book 20: The Incendiary Murders

When the Powys mansion belonging to an ageing rock star is rocked by a deadly explosion, Detective Inspector Yvonne Giles finds herself tasked with a case of murder, suspicion, and secrets. As shockwaves ripple through the community, Giles must pierce the impenetrable facades of the characters surrounding the case, racing the clock to find the culprit and prevent further bombings. With an investigation full of twists and turns, DI Yvonne Giles must unravel the truth before it's too late.

Remember to watch out for Book 21, coming in October, 2023.

Printed in Great Britain
by Amazon

30315208R00101